Robert Browning

Pacchiarotto and how he Worked in Distemper

With other Poems

Robert Browning

Pacchiarotto and how he Worked in Distemper
With other Poems

ISBN/EAN: 9783337158392

Printed in Europe, USA, Canada, Australia, Japan

Cover: Foto ©Andreas Hilbeck / pixelio.de

More available books at **www.hansebooks.com**

PACCHIAROTTO

AND

HOW HE WORKED IN DISTEMPER:

WITH OTHER POEMS.

BY

ROBERT BROWNING.

BOSTON:

JAMES R. OSGOOD AND COMPANY,

(Late Ticknor & Fields, and Fields, Osgood, & Co.

1877.

CONTENTS.

	PAGE
PROLOGUE	9
OF PACCHIAROTTO, AND HOW HE WORKED IN DISTEMPER	11
AT THE 'MERMAID'	43
HOUSE	53
SHOP	57
PISGAH-SIGHTS. 1.	65
" 2.	68
FEARS AND SCRUPLES	72
NATURAL MAGIC	76
MAGICAL NATURE	78

8 *CONTENTS.*

PAGE

BIFURCATION 79

NUMPHOLEPTOS 82

APPEARANCES 90

ST. MARTIN'S SUMMER 91

A FORGIVENESS 98

CENCIAJA 120

FILIPPO BALDINUCCI ON THE PRIVILEGE OF BURIAL . 136

EPILOGUE 166

PACCHIAROTTO

AND OTHER POEMS.

PROLOGUE.

1.

O the old wall here! How I could pass
Life in a long Midsummer day,
My feet confined to a plot of grass,
My eyes from a wall not once away!

2.

And lush and lithe do the creepers clothe
Yon wall I watch, with a wealth of green:
Its bald red bricks draped, nothing loath,
In lappets of tangle they laugh between.

3.

Now, what is it makes pulsate the robe?
Why tremble the sprays? What life o'erbrims
The body, — the house, no eye can probe, —
Divined as, beneath a robe, the limbs?

4.

And there again! But my heart may guess
 Who tripped behind; and she sang perhaps:
So, the old wall throbbed, and its life's excess
 Died out and away in the leafy wraps!

5.

Wall upon wall are between us: life
 And song should away from heart to heart!
I — prison-bird, with a ruddy strife
 At breast, and a lip whence storm-notes start —

6.

Hold on, hope hard in the subtle thing
 That's spirit: though cloistered fast, soar free;
Account as wood, brick, stone, this ring
 Of the rueful neighbors, and — forth to thee!

OF PACCHIAROTTO, AND HOW HE WORKED IN DISTEMPER.

1.

QUERY: was ever a quainter
Crotchet than this of the painter
Giacomo Pacchiarotto
Who took "Reform" for his motto?

2.

He, pupil of old Fungaio,
Is always confounded (heigho!)
With Pacchia, contemporaneous
No question, but how extraneous
In the grace of soul, the power
Of hand, — undoubted dower
Of Pacchia who decked (as *we* know,
My Kirkup!) San Bernardino,

Turning the small dark Oratory
To Siena's Art-laboratory,
As he made its straightness roomy
And glorified its, gloomy,
With Bazzi and Beccafumi.
(Another heigho for Bazzi :
How people miscall. him Razzi !)

3.

This Painter was of opinion
Our; earth, should˙ be, his˙ dominion ,
Whose Art could correct to pattern
What Nature had slurred — the slattern !
And since, beneath the heavens,
Things lay now at, sixes and sevens,
Or, as he, said, *sopra-sotto* —
Thought the painter Pacchiarotto
Things wanted reforming, therefore.
" Wanted it " — ay, but wherefore ?
When earth held one so ready
As he to step forth, stand steady

In the middle of God's creation
And prove to demonstration
What the dark is, what the light is,
What the wrong is, what the right is,
What the ugly, what the beautiful,
What the restive, what the dutiful,
In Mankind profuse around him?
Man, devil as now he found him,
Would presently soar up angel
At the summons of such evangel,
And owe — what would Man *not* owe
To the painter Pacchiarotto?
Ay, look to thy laurels, Giotto!

4.

But Man, he perceived, was stubborn,
Grew regular brute, once cub born ;
And it struck him as expedient —
Ere he tried to make obedient,
By piping advice in one key,
The wolf, fox, bear and monkey —

That his pipe should play a prelude

To something heaven-tinged not hell-hued,

Something not harsh but docile,

Man-liquid, not Man-fossil —

Not fact, in short, but fancy.

By a laudable necromancy

He would conjure up ghosts — a circle

Deprived of the means to work ill

Should his music prove distasteful,

And pearls to the swine go wasteful.

To be rent of swine — that *was* hard !

With fancy he ran no hazard :

Fact might knock him o'er the mazard.

5.

So, the painter Pacchiarotto

Constructed himself a grotto

In the quarter of Stalloreggi —

As authors of note allege ye.

And on each of the whitewashed sides of it

He painted — (none far and wide so fit

As he to perform in fresco) —
He painted nor cried *quiesco*
Till he peopled its every square foot
With Man — from the Beggar barefoot
To the Noble in cap and feather:
All sorts and conditions together.
The Soldier in breastplate and helmet
Stood frowningly — hail fellow well met —
By the Priest armed with bell, book and candle.
Nor did he omit to handle
The Fair Sex, our brave distemperer:
Not merely King, Clown, Pope, Emperor —
He diversified too his Hades
Of all forms, pinched Labor and paid Ease,
With as mixed an assemblage of Ladies.

6.

Which work done, dry, — he rested him,
Cleaned palette, washed brush, divested him
Of the apron that suits *frescanti*,
And, bonnet on ear stuck jaunty,

This hand upon hip well planted,
That, free to wave as it wanted,
He addressed in a choice oration
His folk of each name and nation
On the duties of every station.
The pope was declared an arrant
Impostor at once, I warrant.
The Emperor — truth might tax him
With ignorance of the maxim
" Shear sheep but nowise flay them ! "
And the Vulgar that obey them,
The Ruled, well-matched with the Ruling,
They failed not of wholesome schooling
On their knavery and their fooling.
As for Art — where's decorum ?   Pooh-poohed it is
By Poets that plague us with lewd ditties,
And Painters that pester with nudities !

7.

Now, your rater and debater
Is balked by a mere spectator

Who simply stares and listens
Tongue-tied, while eye nor glistens
Nor brow grows hot and twitchy,
Nor mouth, for a combat itchy,
Quivers with some convincing
Reply — that sets him wincing?
Nay, rather — reply that furnishes
Your debater with just what burnishes
The crest of him, all one triumph,
As you see him rise, hear him cry " Humph!
Convinced am I? This confutes me?
Receive the rejoinder that suits me!
Confutation of vassal for prince meet —
Wherein all the powers that convince meet,
And mash my opponent to mincemeat!"

8.

So, off from his head flies the bonnet,
His hip loses hand planted on it,
While t'other hand, frequent in gesture,
Slinks modestly back beneath vesture,

As, — hop, skip and jump, — he's along with

Those weak ones he late proved so strong with !

Pope, Emperor, lo he's beside them,

Friendly now, who late could not abide them,

King, Clown, Soldier, Priest, Noble, Burgess ;

And his voice, that out-roared Boanerges,

How minikin-mildly it urges

In accents how gentled and gingered

Its word in defence of the injured !

" O call him not culprit, this Pontiff !

Be hard on this Kaiser ye won't if

Ye take into con-si-de-ration

What dangers attend elevation !

The Priest — who expects him to descant

On duty with more zeal and less cant ?

He preaches but rubbish he's reared in.

The Soldier, grown deaf (by the mere din

Of battle) to mercy, learned tippling

And what not of vice while a stripling.

The Lawyer — his lies are conventional.

And as for the Poor Sort — why mention all

Obstructions that leave barred and bolted
Access to the brains of each dolt-head ? "

9.

He ended, you wager ?   Not half !   A bet ?
Precedence to males in the alphabet !
Still, disposed of Man's A. B. C., there's X.
Y. Z. want assistance, — the Fair Sex !
How much may be said in excuse of
Those vanities — males see no use of —
From silk shoe on heel to laced poll's-hood !
What's their frailty beside our own falsehood ?
The boldest, most brazen of . . . trumpets,
How kind can they be to their dumb pets !
Of   their   charms — how   are   most   frank, how   few
        venal !
While as for those charges of Juvenal —
Quæ nemo dixisset in toto
Nisi (ædepol) ore illoto —
He dismissed every charge with an ' *Apage !* '

10.

Then, cocking (in Scotch phrase) his cap a-gee,

Right hand disengaged from the doublet

— Like landlord, in house he had sublet

Resuming of guardianship gestion,

To call tenants' conduct in question —

Hop, skip, jump, to inside from outside

Of chamber, he lords, ladies, louts eyed

With such transformation of visage

As fitted the censor of this age.

No longer an advocate tepid

Of frailty but champion intrepid

Of strength, — not of falsehood but verity, —

He, one after one, with asperity

Stripped bare all the cant-clothed abuses,

Disposed of sophistic excuses,

Forced folly each shift to abandon,

And left vice with no leg to stand on.

So crushing the force he exerted,

That Man · at his foot lay converted !

11.

True — Man bred of paint-pot and mortar !
But why suppose folks of this sort are
More likely to hear and be tractable
Than folks all alive and, in fact, able
To testify promptly by action
Their ardor, and make satisfaction
For misdeeds *non verbis sed factis ?*
" With folks all alive be my practice
Henceforward!   O mortar, paint-pot O,
Farewell to ye ! " cried Pacchiarotto,
" Let only occasion intérpose ! "

12.

It did so : for, pat to the purpose
Through causes I need not examine,
There fell upon Siena a famine.
In vain did the magistrates busily
Seek succor, fetch grain out of Sicily,
Nay, throw mill and bakehouse wide open —

Such misery followed as no pen
Of mine shall depict ye. Faint, fainter,
Waxed hope of relief: so, our painter,
Emboldened by triumph of recency,
How could he do other with decency
Than rush in this strait to the rescue,
Play schoolmaster, point as with fescue
To each and all slips in Man's spelling
The law of the land? — slips now telling
With monstrous effect on the city,
Whose magistrates moved him to pity
As, bound to read law to the letter,
They minded their hornbook no better.

13.

I ought to have told you, at starting,
How certain, who itched to be carting
Abuses away clean and thorough
From Siena, both province and borough,
Had formed themselves into a company
Whose swallow could bolt in a lump any

Obstruction of scruple, provoking
The nicer throat's coughing and choking.
Fit Club, by as fit a name dignified
Of " Freed Ones " — " *Bardotti* " —which signified
" Spare-Horses " that walk by the wagon
The team has to drudge for and drag on.
This notable Club Pacchiarotto
Had joined long since, paid scot and lot to,
As free and accepted " Bardotto."
The Bailiwick watched with no quiet eye
The outrage thus done to society,
And noted the advent especially
Of Pacchiarotto their fresh ally.

14.

These Spare-Horses forthwith assembled :
Neighed words whereat citizens trembled
As oft as the chiefs, in the Square by
The Duomo, proposed a way whereby
The city were cured of disaster.
" Just substitute servant for master,

Make Poverty Wealth and Wealth Poverty,
Unloose Man from overt and covert tie,
And straight out of social confusion
True Order would spring !"   Brave illusion —
Aims heavenly attained by means earthy !

15.

Off to these at full speed rushed our worthy, —
Brain practised and tongue no less tutored,
In argument's armor accoutred, —
Sprang forth, mounted rostrum and essayed
Proposals like those to which "Yes" said
So glibly each personage painted
O'. the wall-side wherewith you're acquainted.
He harangued on the faults of the Bailiwick:
"Red soon were our State-candle's paly wick,
If wealth would become but interfluous,
Fill voids up with just the superfluous ;
If ignorance gave way to knowledge
— Not pedantry picked up at college
From Doctors, Professors *et cætera* —

(*They* say : '*kai ta loipa* ' —like better a
Long Greek string of *kappas, taus, lambdas,*
Tacked on to the tail of each damned ass) —
No knowledge we want of this quality,
But knowledge indeed — practicality
Through insight's fine universality !
If you shout ' *Bailiffs, out on ye all ! Fie,*
Thou Chief of our forces, Amalfi,
Who shieldest the rogue and the clotpoll ! '
If you pounce on and poke out, with what pole
I leave ye to fancy, our Siena's
Beast-litter of sloths and hyenas — "
(Whoever to scan this is ill able
Forgets the town's name's a dissyllable)
"If, this done, ye did — as ye might — place
For once the right man in the right place,
If you listened to me . . ."

16.

At which last " If "
There flew at his throat like a mastiff

One Spare-Horse — another and another!
Such outbreak of tumult and pother,
Horse-faces a-laughing and fleering,
Horse-voices a-mocking and jeering,
Horse-hands raised to collar the caitiff
Whose impudence ventured the late "If" —
That, had not fear sent Pacchiarotto
Off tramping, as fast as could trot toe,
Away from the scene of discomfiture —
Had he stood there stock-still in a dumb fit — sure
Am I he had paid in his person
Till his mother might fail to know her son,
Though she gazed on him never so wistful,
In the figure so tattered and tristful.
Each mouth full of curses, each fist full
Of cuffings — behold, Pacchiarotto,
The pass which thy project has got to,
Of trusting, nigh ashes still hot — tow!
(The paraphrase — which I much need — is
From Horace *'per ignes incedis.'*)

17.

Right and left did he dash helter-skelter
In agonized search of a shelter.
No purlieu so blocked and no alley
So blind as allowed him to rally
His spirits and see — nothing hampered
IIis steps if he trudged and not scampered
Up here and down there in a city
That's all ups and downs, more the pity
For folks who would outrun the constable.
At last he stopped short at the one stable
And sure place of refuge that's offered
Humanity. Lately was coffered
A corpse in its sepulchre, situate
By St. John's Observance. "Habituate
Thyself to the strangest of bedfellows,
And, kicked by the live, kiss the dead fellows!"
So Misery counselled the craven.
At once he crept safely to haven
Through a hole left unbricked in the structure.
Ay, Misery, in have you tucked your

Poor client and left him conterminous
With — pah ! — the thing fetid and verminous !
(I gladly would spare you the detail,
But History writes what I retail.)

18.

Two days did he groan in his domicile :
"Good Saints, set me free and I promise I'll
Abjure all ambition of preaching
Change, whether to minds touched by teaching
— The smooth folk of fancy, mere figments
Created by plaster and pigments, —
Or to minds that receive with such rudeness
Dissuasion from pride, greed and lewdness,
— The rough folk of fact, life's true specimens
Of mind — '*haud in posse sed esse mens*'
As it was, is and shall be forever
Despite of my utmost endeavor.
O live foes I thought to illumine,
Henceforth lie untroubled your gloom in !
I need my own light, every spark, as
I couch with this sole friend — a carcass !"

19.

Two days thus he maundered and rambled;
Then, starved back to sanity, scrambled
From out his receptacle loathsome.
" A spectre ! " — declared upon oath some
Who saw him emerge and (appalling
To mention) his garments a-crawling
With plagues far beyond the Egyptian.
He gained, in a state past description
A convent of monks, the Observancy.

20.

Thus far is a fact : I reserve fancy
For Fancy's more proper employment :
And now she waves wing with enjoyment,
To tell ye how preached the Superior
When somewhat our painter's exterior
Was sweetened. He needed (no mincing
The matter) much soaking and rinsing,
Nay, rubbing with drugs odoriferous,

Till, rid of his garments pestiferous
And robed by the help of the Brotherhood
In odds and ends, — this gown and t'other hood, —
His empty inside first well-garnished, —
He delivered a tale round, unvarnished.

21.

" Ah, Youth ! " so might run the admonishment,
"Thine error scarce moves my astonishment.
For — why shall I shrink from asserting? —
Myself have had hopes of converting
The foolish to wisdom, till, sober,
My life found its May grow October.
I talked and I wrote, but, one morning,
Life's Autumn bore fruit in this warning :
' *Let tongue rest, and quiet thy quill be !*
Earth is earth and not heaven, and ne'er will be.'
Man's work is to labor and leaven —
As best he may — earth here with heaven ;
'Tis work for work's sake that he's needing:
Let him work on and on as if speeding

Work's end, but not dream of succeeding!

Because if success were intended,

Why, heaven would begin ere earth ended.

A Spare-Horse? Be rather a thill-horse,

Or — what's the plain truth — just a mill-horse!

Earth's a mill where we grind and wear mufflers :

A whip awaits shirkers and shufflers

Who slacken their pace, sick of lugging

At what don't advance for their tugging.

Though round goes the mill, we must still post

On and on as if moving the mill-post.

So, grind away, mouth-wise and pen-wise,

Do all that we can to make men wise!

And if men prefer to be foolish,

Ourselves have proved horse-like not mulish :

Sent grist, a good sackful, to hopper,

And worked as the Master thought proper.

Tongue I wag, pen I ply, who am Abbot ;

Stick, thou, Son, to paint-brush and dab-pot!

But, soft! I scratch hard on the scab hot ?

Though cured of thy plague, there may linger

A pimple I fray with rough finger ?
So soon could my homily transmute
Thy brass into gold ?   Why, the man's mute ! "

22.

" Ay, Father, I'm mute with admiring
How Nature's indulgence untiring
Still bids us turn deaf ear to Reason's
Best rhetoric — clutch at all seasons
And hold fast to what's proved untenable !
Thy maxim is — Man's not amenable
To argument : whereof by consequence —
Thine arguments reach me : a non-sequence !
Yet blush not discouraged, O Father !
I stand unconverted, the rather
That nowise I need a conversion.
No live man (I cap thy assertion)
By argument ever could take hold
Of me.   'Twas the dead thing, the clay-cold,
Which grinned *' Art thou so in a hurry*
That out of warm light thou must scurry

And join me down here in the dungeon
Because, above, one's Jack and one — John,
One's swift in the race, one — a hobbler,
One's a crowned king and one — a capped cobbler,
Rich and poor, sage and fool, virtuous, vicious?
Why complain? Art thou so unsuspicious
That all's for an hour of essaying
Who's fit and who's unfit for playing
His part in the after-construction
— Heaven's Piece whereof Earth's the Induction?
Things rarely go smooth at Rehearsal.
Wait patient the change universal,
And act, and let act, in existence!
For, as thou art clapped hence or hissed hence,
Thou hast thy promotion or otherwise.
And why must wise thou have thy brother wise
Because in rehearsal thy cue be
To shine by the side of a booby?
No polishing garnet to ruby!
All's well that ends well — through Art's magic.
Some end, whether comic or tragic,

The Artist has purposed, be certain!
Explained at the fall of the curtain —
In showing thy wisdom at odds with
That folly: he tries men and gods with
No problem for weak wits to solve meant,
But one worth such Author's evolvement.
So, back nor disturb play's production
By giving thy brother instruction
To throw up his fool's-part allotted!
Lest haply thyself prove besotted
When stript, for thy pains, of that costume
Of sage, which has bred the imposthume
I prick to relieve thee of, — Vanity!'

23.

" So, Father, behold me in sanity!
I'm back to the paint-brush and mahlstick:
And as for Man — let each and all stick
To what was prescribed them at starting!
Once planted as fools — no departing

From folly one inch, *sæculorum*
In sæcula! Pass me the jorum,
And push me the platter — my stomach
Retains, through its fasting, still some ache —
And then, with your kind *Benedicite*,
Good-by!"

24.

I have told with simplicity
My tale, dropped those harsh analytics,
And tried to content you, my critics,
Who greeted my early uprising!
I knew you through all the disguising,
Droll dogs, as I jumped up, cried "Heyday
This Monday is — what else but May-day
And these in the drabs, blues and yellows
Are surely the privileged fellows.
So, saltbox and bones, tongs and bellows!"
(I threw up the window) "Your pleasure?"

25.

Then he who directed the measure —
An old friend — put leg forward nimbly,
"We critics as sweeps out your chimbly!
Much soot to remove from your flue sir!
Who spares coal in kitchen an't you, sir!
And neighbors complain it's no joke, sir,
— You ought to consume your own smoke, sir!"

26.

Ah, rogues, but my housemaid suspects you —
Is confident oft she detects you
In bringing more filth into my house
Than ever you found there! I'm pious
However: 'twas God made you dingy
And me — with no need to be stingy
Of soap, when 'tis sixpence the packet.
So, dance away, boys, dust my jacket,
Bang drum and blow fife — ay, and rattle
Your brushes, for that's half the battle!

Don't trample the grass, — hocus-pocus
With grime my Spring snow-drop and crocus, —
And, what with your rattling and tinkling,
Who knows but you give me an inkling
How music sounds, thanks to the jangle
Of regular drum and triangle?
Whereby, tap-tap, chink-chink, 'tis proven
I break rule as bad as Beethoven.
" That chord now — a groan or a grunt is't?
Schumann's self was no worse contrapuntist.
No ear! or if ear, so tough-gristled —
He thought that he sung while he whistled!"

27.

So, this time I whistle, not sing at all,
My story, the largess I fling at all
And every the rough there whose *aubade*
Did its best to amuse me, — nor *so* bad!
Take my thanks, pick up largess, and scamper
Off free, ere your mirth gets a damper!

You've Monday, your one day, your fun-day,

While mine is a year that's all Sunday.

I've seen you, times — who knows how many? —

Dance in here, strike up, play the zany,

Make mouths at the Tenant, hoot warning

You'll find him decamped next May-morning;

Then scuttle away, glad to 'scape hence

With — kicks? no, but laughter and ha'pence!

Mine's freehold, by grace of the grand Lord

Who lets out the ground here, — my landlord:

To him I pay quit-rent — devotion;

Nor hence shall I budge, I've a notion,

Nay, here shall my whistling and singing

Set all his street's echoes a-ringing

Long after the last of your number

Has ceased my front-court to encumber

While, treading down rose and ranunculus,

You *Tommy-make-room-for-your-Uncle* us!

Troop, all of you — man or homunculus,

Quick march! for Xanthippe, my housemaid,

If once on your pates she a souse made

With what, pan or pot, bowl or *skoramis*
First comes to her hand — things were more amiss!
I would not for worlds be your place in —
Recipient of slops from the basin!
You, Jack-in-the-Green, leaf-and-twiggishness
Won't save a dry thread on your priggishness!
While as for Quilp-Hop-o'-my-thumb there,
Banjo-Byron that twangs the strum-strum there —
He'll think, as the pickle he curses,
I've discharged on his pate his own verses!
" Dwarfs are saucy," says Dickens : so, sauced in
Your own sauce, . . .*

28.

But, back to my Knight of the Pencil,
Dismissed to his fresco and stencil!
Whose story — begun with a chuckle,
And throughout timed by raps of the knuckle, —

---

* No, please! For
  " Who would be satirical
   On a thing so very small ? "— PRINTER'S DEVIL.

To small enough purpose were studied
If it ends with crown cracked or nose bloodied.
Come, critics, — not shake hands, excuse me !
But — say have you grudged to amuse me
This once in the forty-and-over
Long years since you trampled my clover
And scared from my house-eaves each sparrow
I never once harmed by that arrow
Of song, *karterotaton belos*,
(Which Pindar declares the true *melos*)
I was forging and filing and finishing,
And no whit my labors diminishing
Because, though high up in a chamber
Where none of your kidney may clamber
Your hullabaloo would approach me ?
Was it "grammar" wherein you would "coach" me —
You, — pacing in even that paddock
Of language allotted you *ad hoc*,
With a clog at your fetlocks, — you — scorners
Of me free of all its four corners ?
Was it "clearness of words which convey thought ?"

Ay, if words never needed enswathe aught
But ignorance, impudence, envy
And malice — what word-swathe would then vie
With yours for a clearness crystalline ?
But had you to put in one small line
Some thought big and bouncing — as noddle
Of goose, born to cackle and waddle
And bite at man's heel as goose-wont is,
Never felt plague its puny *os frontis* —
You'd know, as you hissed, spat and sputtered,
Clear "quack-quack" is easily uttered !

29.

Lo, I've laughed out my laugh on this mirth-day !
Beside, at week's end, dawns my birth-day,
That *hebdome, hieron emar* —
(More things in a day than you deem are !)
— *Tei gar Apollona chrusaora*
Egeinato Leto. So, gray or ray
Betide me, six days hence, I'm vexed here

By no sweep, that's certain, till next year!

"Vexed?"— roused from what else were insipid ease!

Leave snoring a-bed to Pheidippides!

We'll up and work! won't we, Euripides?

AT THE 'MERMAID.'

The figure that thou here seest . . Tut!
Was it for gentle Shakespeare put?

B. JONSON. (*Adapted.*)

I.

I — "Next Poet?"   No, my hearties,
    I nor am nor fain would be!
Choose your chiefs and pick your parties,
    Not one soul revolt to me!
I, forsooth, sow song sedition?
    I, a schism in verse provoke?
I, blown up by bard's ambition,
    Burst — your bubble-king?   You joke.

2.

Come, be grave!   The sherris mantling
    Still about each mouth, mayhap,
Breeds you insight — just a scantling —
    Brings me truth out — just a scrap.

Look and tell me ! Written, spoken,
    Here's my life-long work : and where
— Where's your warrant or my token
    I'm the dead king's son and heir ?

3.

Here's my work : does work discover
    What was rest from work — my life ?
Did I live man's hater, lover ?
    Leave the world at peace, at strife ?
Call earth ugliness or beauty ?
    See things there in large or small ?
Use to pay its Lord my duty ?
    Use to own a lord at all ?

4.

Blank of such a record, truly,
    Here's the work I hand, this scroll,
Yours to take or leave ; as duly,
    Mine remains the unproffered soul.

So much, no whit more, my debtors —
How should one like me lay claim
To that largess elders, betters
Sell you cheap their souls for — fame ?

5.

Which of you did I enable
Once to slip inside my breast
There to catalogue and label
What I like least, what love best,
Hope and fear, believe and doubt of,
Seek and shun, respect — deride ?
Who has right to make a rout of
Rarities he found inside ?

6.

Rarities or, as he'd rather,
Rubbish such as stocks his own :
Need and greed (O strange) the Father
Fashioned not for him alone !

Whence — the comfort set a-strutting,
  Whence — the outcry "Haste, behold !
Bard's breast open wide, past shutting,
  Shows what brass we took for gold ! "

7.

Friends, I doubt not he'd display you
  Brass — myself call oreichalch, —
Furnish much amusement ; pray you
  Therefore, be content I balk
Him and you, and bar my portal !
  Here's my work outside : opine
What's inside me mean and mortal !
  Take your pleasure, leave me mine !

8.

Which is — not to buy your laurel
  As last king did, nothing loath.
Tale adorned and pointed moral
  Gained him praise and pity both.

Out rushed sighs and groans by dozens,
    Forth by scores oaths, curses flew:
Proving you were cater-cousins,
    Kith and kindred, king and you!

9.

Whereas do I ne'er so little
    (Thanks to sherris) leave ajar
Bosom's gate — no jot nor tittle
    Grow we nearer than we are.
Sinning, sorrowing, despairing,
    Body-ruined, spirit-wrecked, —
Should I give my woes an airing, —
    Where's one plague that claims respect?

10.

Have you found your life distasteful?
    My life did and does smack sweet.
Was your youth of pleasure wasteful?
    Mine I saved and hold complete.

Do your joys with age diminish?
  When mine fail me, I'll complain.
Must in death your daylight finish?
  My sun sets to rise again.

11.

What, like you, he proved — your Pilgrim —
  This our world a wilderness,
Earth still gray and heaven still grim,
  Not a hand there his might press,
Not a heart his own might throb to,
  Men all rogues and women — say,
Dolls which boys' heads duck and bob to,
  Grown folk drop or throw away?

12.

My experience being other,
  How should I contribute verse
Worthy of your king and brother?
  Balaam-like I bless, not curse.

I find earth not gray but rosy,
  Heaven not grim but fair of hue.
Do I stoop? I pluck a posy.
  Do I stand and stare? All's blue.

13.

Doubtless I am pushed and shoved by
  Rogues and fools enough : the more
Good luck mine, I love, am loved by
  Some few honest to the core.
Scan the near high, scout the far low !
  "But the low come close : " what then ?
Simpletons? My match is Marlowe ;
  Sciolists? My mate is Ben.

14.

Womankind — "the cat-like nature,
  False and fickle, vain and weak " —
What of this sad nomenclature
  Suits my tongue, if I must speak?

Does the sex invite, repulse so,
    Tempt, betray, by fits and starts?
So becalm but to convulse so,
    Decking heads and breaking hearts?

15.

Well may you blaspheme at fortune!
    I " threw Venus " (Ben, expound!)
Never did I need importune
    Her, of all the Olympian round.
Blessings on my benefactress!
    Cursings suit — for aught I know —
Those who twitched her by the back tress,
    Tugged and thought to turn her — so!

16.

Therefore, since no leg to stand on
    Thus I'm left with, — joy or grief
Be the issue, — I abandon
    Hope or care you name me Chief!

Chief and king and Lord's anointed,

   I? — who never once have wished

Death before the day appointed:

   Lived and liked, not poohed and pished!

17.

"Ah, but so I shall not enter,

   Scroll in hand, the common heart —

Stopped at surface: since at centre

   Song should reach *Welt-schmerz*, world-smart!"

"Enter in the heart?" Its shelly

   Cuirass guard mine, fore and aft!

Such song "enters in the belly

   And is cast out in the draught."

18.

Back then to our sherris-brewage!

   "Kingship" quotha? I shall wait —

Waive the present time: some new age . . .

   But let fools anticipate!

Meanwhile greet me — "friend, good fellow,
Gentle Will," my merry men !
As for making Envy yellow
With "Next Poet" — (Manners, Ben !)

HOUSE.

1.

SHALL I sonnet-sing you about myself?
Do I live in a house you would like to see?
Is it scant of gear, has it store of pelf?
"Unlock my heart with a sonnet-key?"

2.

Invite the world, as my betters have done?
"Take notice : this building remains on view,
Its suites of reception every one,
Its private apartment and bedroom too ;

3.

"For a ticket, apply to the Publisher."
No : thanking the public, I must decline.
A peep through my window, if folks prefer ;
But, please you, no foot over threshold of mine !

4.

I have mixed with a crowd and heard free talk
  In a foreign land where an earthquake chanced
And a house stood gaping, nought to balk
  Man's eye wherever he gazed or glanced.

5.

The whole of the frontage shaven sheer,
  The inside gaped : exposed to day,
Right and wrong and common and queer,
  Bare, as the palm of your hand, it lay.

6.

The owner? Oh, he had been crushed, no doubt!
  "Odd tables and chairs for a man of wealth!
What a parcel of musty old books about!
  He smoked, — no wonder he lost his health!

7.

" I doubt if he bathed before he dressed.

A brazier ? — the pagan, he burned perfumes!

You see it is proved, what the neighbors guessed :

His wife and himself had separate rooms."

8.

Friends, the goodman of the house at least

Kept house to himself till an earthquake came :

'Tis the fall of its frontage permits you feast

On the inside arrangement you praise or blame.

9.

Outside should suffice for evidence :

And whoso desires to penetrate

Deeper, must dive by the spirit-sense —

No optics like yours, at any rate!

10.

" Hoity toity !   A street to explore,

Your house the exception !   '*With this same key*
Shakespeare unlocked his heart,' once more ! "

Did Shakespeare ?   If so, the less Shakespeare he !

SHOP.

1.

So, friend, your shop was all your house !
Its front, astonishing the street,
Invited view from man and mouse
  To what diversity of treat
  Behind its glass — the single sheet !

2.

What gimcracks, genuine Japanese :
  Gape-jaw and goggle-eye, the frog ;
Dragons, owls, monkeys, beetles, geese ;
  Some crush-nosed human-hearted dog :
  Queer names, too, such a catalogue !

3.

I thought " And he who owns ˙ the wealth
Which blocks the window's vastitude,
— Ah, could I peep at him by stealth
Behind his ware, pass shop, intrude
On house itself, what scenes were viewed !

4.

" If wide and showy thus the shop,
What must the habitation prove ?
The true house with no name a-top —
The mansion, distant one remove,
Once get him off his traffic-grove !

5.

" Pictures he likes, or books perhaps ;
And as for buying most and best,
Commend me to these city chaps !
Or else he's social, takes his rest
On Sundays, with a Lord for guest.

6.

" Some suburb-palace, parked about
  And gated grandly, built last year :
The four-mile walk to keep off gout ;
  Or big seat sold by bankrupt peer :
  But then he takes the rail, that's clear.

7.

" Or, stop ! I wager, taste selects
  Some out o' the way, some all-unknown
Retreat : the neighborhood suspects
  Little that he who rambles lone
  Makes Rothschild tremble on his throne ! "

8.

Nowise ! Nor Mayfair residence
  Fit to receive and entertain, —
Nor Hampstead villa's kind defence
  From noise and crowd, from dust and drain, —
  Nor country-box was soul's domain !

9.

Nowise! At back of all that spread
Of merchandise, woe's me, I find
A hole i' the wall where, heels by head,
 The owner couched, his ware behind,
 — In cupboard suited to his mind.

10.

For why? He saw no use of life
 But, while he drove a roaring trade,
To chuckle " Customers are rife ! "
 To chafe " So much hard cash outlaid
 Yet zero in my profits made !

11.

" This novelty costs pains, but — takes ?
 Cumbers my counter ! Stock no more !
This article, no such great shakes,
 Fizzes like wild fire ? Underscore
 The cheap thing — thousands to the fore ! "

12.

'Twas lodging best to live most nigh
(Cramp, coffinlike as crib might be)
Receipt of Custom ; ear and eye
    Wanted no outworld : " Hear and see
    The bustle in the shop ! " quoth he.

13.

My fancy of a merchant-prince
    Was different.   Through his wares we groped
Our darkling way to — not to mince
    The matter — no black den where moped
    The master if we interloped !

14.

Shop was shop only : household-stuff ?
    What did he want with comforts there ?
" Walls, ceiling, floor, stay blank and rough,
    So goods on sale show rich and rare !
    ' *Sell and scud home*,' be shop's affair ! "

15. .

What might he deal in? Gems, suppose !
Since somehow business must be done
At cost of trouble, — see, he throws
  You choice of jewels, every one
  Good, better, best, star, moon and sun !

16.

Which lies within your power of purse ?
  This ruby that would tip aright
Solomon's sceptre? Oh, your nurse
  Wants simply coral, the delight
  Of teething baby, — stuff to bite !

17.

Howe'er your choice fell, straight you took
  Your purchase, prompt your money rang
On counter, — scarce the man forsook
  His study of the " Times," just swang
  Till-ward his hand that stopped the clang, —

18.

Then off made buyer with a prize,
Then seller to his " Times " returned,
And so did day wear, wear, till eyes
Brightened apace, for rest was earned :
He locked door long ere candle burned.

19.

And whither went he ? Ask himself,
Not me ! To change of scene, I think.
Once sold the ware and pursed the pelf,
Chaffer was scarce his meat and drink,
Nor all his music — money-chink.

20.

Because a man has shop to mind
In time and place, since flesh must live,
Needs spirit lack all life behind,
All stray thoughts, fancies fugitive,
All loves except what trade can give ?

21.

I want to know a butcher paints,

A baker rhymes for his pursuit,

Candlestick-maker much acquaints

His soul with song, or, haply mute,

Blows out his brains upon the flute!

22.

But — shop each day and all day long!

Friend, your good angel slept, your star

Suffered eclipse, fate did you wrong!

From where these sorts of treasures are,

There should our hearts be — Christ, how far!

PISGAH–SIGHTS. I.

I.

OVER the ball of it,
  Peering and prying,
How I see all of it,
  Life there, outlying!
Roughness and smoothness,
  Shine and defilement,
Grace and uncouthness:
  One reconcilement.

2.

Orbed as appointed,
  Sister with brother
Joins, ne'er disjointed
  One from the other.

All's lend-and-borrow;
· Good, see, wants evil,
Joy demands sorrow,
Angel weds devil !

3.

"Which things must — *why* be ? "
Vain our endeavor !
So shall things aye be
As they were ever.
"Such things should *so* be ! "
Sage our desistence !
Rough-smooth let globe be,
Mixed — man's existence !

4.

Man — wise and foolish,
Lover and scorner,
Docile and mulish —
Keep each his corner !

Honey yet gall of it!
There's the life lying,
And I see all of it,
Only, I'm dying!

PISGAH-SIGHTS. 2.

1.

COULD I but live again,
  Twice my life over,
Would I once strive again?
  Would not I cover
Quietly all of it —
  Greed and ambition —
So, from the pall of it,
  Pass to fruition?

2.

" Soft ! " I'd say, " Soul mine !
  Three-score and ten years,
Let the blind mole mine
  Digging out deniers !

Let the dazed hawk soar,
  Claim the sun's rights too !
Turf 'tis thy walk's o'er,
  Foliage thy flight's to."

3.

Only a learner,
  Quick one or slow one,
Just a discerner,
  I would teach no one.
I am earth's native :
  No re-arranging it !
I be creative,
  Chopping and changing it ?

4.

March, men, my fellows !
  Those who, above me,
(Distance so mellows)
  Fancy you love me :

Those who, below me,

   (Distance makes great so)

Free to forego me,

   Fancy you hate so !

5.

Praising, reviling,

   Worst head and best head,

Past me defiling,

   Never arrested,

Wanters, abounders,

   March, in gay mixture,

Men, my surrounders !   .

   I am the fixture.

6.

So shall I fear thee,

   Mightiness yonder !

Mock-sun — more near thee,

   What is to wonder ?

So shall I love thee,
　Down in the dark, — lest
Glowworm I prove thee,
　Star that now sparklest!

FEARS AND SCRUPLES.

1.

HERE'S my case. Of old I used to love him,
  This same unseen friend, before I knew:
Dream there was none like him, none above him, —
  Wake to hope and trust my dream was true.

2.

Loved I not his letters full of beauty?
  Not his actions famous far and wide?
Absent, he would know I vowed him duty,
  Present, he would find me at his side.

3.

Pleasant fancy! for I had but letters,
  Only knew of actions by hearsay:
He himself was busied with my betters;
  What of that? My turn must come some day.

4.

"Some day" proving — no day! Here's the puzzle.
    Passed and passed my turn is. Why complain?
He's so busied! If I could but muzzle
    People's foolish mouths that give me pain !

5.

"Letters?" (hear them !) "You a judge of writing?
    Ask the experts! How they shake the head
O'er these characters, your friend's inditing —
    Call them forgery from A. to Z. !

6.

"Actions? Where's your certain proof" (they bother)
    "He, of all you find so great and good,
He, he only, claims this, that, the other
    Action — claimed by men, a multitude?"

7.

I can simply wish I might refute you,
    Wish my friend would, — by a word, a wink, —
Bid me stop that foolish mouth, — you brute you!
    He keeps absent, — why, I cannot think.

8.

Never mind! Though foolishness may flout me,
  One thing's sure enough: 'tis neither frost,
No, nor fire, shall freeze or burn from out me
  Thanks for truth — though falsehood, gained —
    though lost.

9.

All my days, I'll go the softlier, sadlier,
  For that dream's sake! How forget the thrill
Through and through me as I thought "The gladlier
  Lives my friend because I love him still!"

10.

Ah, but there's a menace some one utters!
  "What and if your friend at home play tricks?
Peep at hide-and-seek behind the shutters?
  Mean your eyes should pierce through solid bricks?

11.

"What and if he, frowning, wake you, dreamy
  Lay on you the blame that bricks — conceal?
Say '*At least I saw who did not see me,*
  Does see now, and presently shall feel?'"

12.

"Why, that makes your friend a monster!" say you:
"Had his house no window?   At first nod,
Would you not have hailed him?"   Hush, I pray
   you !
What if this friend happen to be — God ?

NATURAL MAGIC.

I.

ALL I can say is — I saw it !

The room was as bare as your hand.

I locked in the swarth little lady, — I swear,

From the head to the foot of her — well, quite as
bare !

"No Nautch shall cheat me," said I, "taking my
stand

At this bolt which I draw !" And this bolt — I
withdraw it,

And there laughs the lady, not bare, but embowered

With — who knows what verdure, o'erfruited, o'er-
flowered ?

Impossible ! Only — I saw it !

2.

All I can sing is — I feel it !

This life was as blank as that room ;

I let you pass in here. Precaution, indeed ?

Walls, ceiling and floor, — not a chance for a weed !

Wide opens the entrance : where's cold now, where's
  gloom ?

No May to sow seed here, no June to reveal it,

Behold you enshrined in these blooms of your bringing,

These fruits of your bearing — nay, birds of your
  winging !

A fairy-tale ! Only — I feel it !

MAGICAL NATURE.

1.

FLOWER — I never fancied, jewel — I profess you !
Bright I see and soft I feel the outside of a
flower.
Save but glow inside and — jewel, I should guess
you,
Dim to sight and rough to touch : the glory is
the dower.

2.

You, forsooth, a flower? Nay, my love, a jewel —
Jewel at no mercy of a moment in your prime !
Time may fray the flower-face : kind be time or
cruel,
Jewel, from each facet, flash your laugh at time !

BIFURCATION.

WE were two lovers ; let .me lie by her,
My tomb beside her tomb. On hers inscribe —
"I loved him ; but my reason bade prefer
Duty to love, reject the tempter's bribe
Of rose and lily when each path diverged,
And either I must pace to life's far end
As love should lead me, or, as duty urged,
Plod the worn causeway arm in arm with friend.
So, truth turned falsehood : '*How I loathe a flower,
How prize the pavement !*' still caressed his car —
The deafish friend's — through life's day, hour by
    hour,
As he laughed (coughing) '*Ay, it would appear !*'
But deep within my heart of hearts there hid
Ever the confidence, amends for all,
That heaven repairs what wrong earth's journey did,
When love from life-long exile comes at call.

Duty and love, one broadway, were the best —
Who doubts? But one or other was to choose.
I chose the darkling half, and wait the rest
In that new world where light and darkness fuse."

Inscribe on mine — "I loved her : love's track lay
O'er sand and pebble, as all travellers know.
Duty led through a smiling country, gay
With greensward where the rose and lily blow.
'*Our roads are diverse: farewell, love!*' said she :
"*'Tis duty I abide by: homely sward*
And not the rock-rough picturesque for me!
Above, where both roads join, I wait reward.
Be you as constant to the path whereon
I leave you planted!' But man needs must move,
Keep moving — whither, when the star is gone
Whereby he steps secure nor strays from love?
No stone but I was tripped by, stumbling-block
But brought me to confusion. Where I fell,
There I lay flat, if moss disguised the rock,
Thence, if flint pierced, I rose and cried '*All's well!*

Duty be mine to tread in that high sphere
Where love from duty ne'er disparts, I trust,
And two halves make that whole, whereof — since here
One must suffice a man — why, this one must!' "

Inscribe each tomb thus : then, some sage acquaint
The simple — which holds sinner, which holds saint!

NUMPHOLEPTOS.

STILL you stand, still you listen, still you smile!
Still melts your moonbeam through me, white awhile,
Softening, sweetening, till sweet and soft
Increase so round this heart of mine, that oft
I could believe your moonbeam-smile has past
The pallid limit and, transformed at last,
Lies, sunlight and salvation — warms the soul
It sweetens, softens!   Would you pass that goal,
Gain love's birth at the limit's happier verge,
And, where an iridescence lurks, but urge
The hesitating pallor on to prime   ·
Of dawn! — true blood-streaked, sun-warmth, action-
time,
By heart-pulse ripened to a ruddy glow
Of gold above my clay — I scarce should know

From gold's self, thus suffused! For gold means
   love.
What means the sad slow silver smile above
My clay but pity, pardon?—at the best,
But acquiescence that I take my rest,
Contented to be clay, while in your heaven
The sun reserves love for the Spirit-Seven
Companioning God's throne they lamp before,
— Leaves earth a mute waste only wandered o'er
By that pale soft sweet disempassioned moon
Which smiles me slow forgiveness! Such, the boon
I beg? Nay, dear, submit to this — just this
Supreme endeavor! As my lips now kiss
Your feet, my arms convulse your shrouding robe,
My eyes, acquainted with the dust, dare probe
Your eyes above for — what, if born, would blind
Mine with redundant bliss, as flash may find
The inert nerve, sting awake the palsied limb,
Bid with life's ecstasy sense overbrim
And suck back death in the resurging joy —
Love, the love whole and sole without alloy!

Vainly! The promise withers! I employ
Lips, arms, eyes, pray the prayer which finds the
    word,
Make the appeal which must be felt, not heard,
And none the more is changed your calm regard:
Rather, its sweet and soft grow harsh and hard —
Forbearance, then repulsion, then disdain.
Avert the rest! I rise, see! — make, again
Once more, the old departure for some track
Untried yet through a world which brings me back
Ever thus fruitlessly to find your feet,
To fix your eyes, to pray the soft and sweet
Which smile there — take from his new pilgrimage
Your outcast, once your inmate, and assuage
With love — not placid pardon now — his thirst
For a mere drop from out the ocean erst
He drank at! Well, the quest shall be renewed.
Fear nothing! Though I linger, unimbued
With any drop, my lips thus close. I go!
So did I leave you, I have found you so,
And doubtlessly, if fated to return,

So shall my pleading persevere and earn
Pardon — not love in that same smile, I learn,
And lose the meaning of, to learn once more,
Vainly !

What fairy track do I explore ?
What magic hall return to, like the gem .
Centuply-angled o'er a diadem ?
You dwell there, hearted ; from your midmost home
Rays forth — through that fantastic world I roam
Ever — from centre to circumference,
Shaft upon colored shaft : this crimsons thence,
That purples out its precinct through the waste.
Surely I had your sanction when I faced,
Fared forth upon that untried yellow ray
Whence I retrack my steps ? They end to-day
Where they began, before your feet, beneath
Your eyes, your smile : the blade is shut in sheath,
Fire quenched in flint ; irradiation, late
Triumphant through the distance, finds its fate,
Merged in your blank pure soul, alike the source

And tomb of that prismatic glow: divorce
Absolute, all-conclusive! Forth I fared,
Treading the lambent flamelet: little cared
If now its flickering took the topaz tint,
If now my dull-caked path gave sulphury hint
Of subterranean rage — no stay nor stint
To yellow, since you sanctioned that I bathe,
Burnish me, soul and body, swim and swathe
In yellow license. Here I reek suffused
With crocus, saffron, orange, as I used
With scarlet, purple, every dye o' the bow
Born of the storm-cloud. As before, you show
Scarce recognition, no approval, some
Mistrust, more wonder at a man become
Monstrous in garb, nay — flesh disguised as well,
Through his adventure. Whatsoe'er befell,
I followed, wheresoe'er it wound, that vein
You authorized should leave your whiteness, stain
Earth's sombre stretch beyond your midmost place
Of vantage, — trode that tinct whereof the trace
On garb and flesh repel you! Yes, I plead

Your own permission — your command, indeed,
That who would worthily retain the love
Must share the knowledge shrined those eyes above,
Go boldly on adventure, break through bounds
O' the quintessential whiteness that surrounds
Your feet, obtain experience of each tinge
That bickers forth to broaden out, impinge
Plainer his foot its pathway all distinct
From every other. Ah, the wonder, linked
With fear, as exploration manifests
What agency it was first tipped the crests
Of unnamed wildflower, soon protruding grew
Portentous mid the sands, as when his hue
Betrays him and the burrowing snake gleams
    through ;
Till, last . . but why parade more shame and pain?
Are not the proofs upon me ? Here again
I pass into your presence, I receive
Your smile of pity, pardon, and I leave . . .
No, not this last of times I leave you, mute,
Submitted to my penance, so my foot

May yet again adventure, tread, from source
To issue, one more ray of rays which course
Each other, at your bidding, from the sphere
Silver and sweet, their birthplace, down that drear
Dark of the world,—you promise shall return
Your pilgrim jewelled as with drops o' the urn
The rainbow paints from, and no smatch at all
Of ghastliness at edge of some cloud-pall
Heaven cowers before, as earth awaits the fall
O' the bolt and flash of doom. Who trusts your
      word
Tries the adventure: and returns—absurd
As frightful—in that sulphur-steeped disguise
Mocking the priestly cloth-of-gold, sole prize
The arch-heretic was wont to bear away
Until he reached the burning. No, I say:
No fresh adventure! No more seeking love
At end of toil, and finding, calm above
My passion, the old statuesque regard,
The sad petrifiç smile!

O you — less hard
And hateful than mistaken and obtuse
Unreason of a she-intelligence !
You very woman with the pert pretence
To match the male achievement ! Like enough !
Ay, you were easy victors, did the rough
Straightway efface itself to smooth, the gruff
Grind down and grow a whisper, — did man's truth
Subdue, for sake of chivalry and ruth,
Its rapier-edge to suit the bulrush-spear
Womanly falsehood fights with ! O that ear
All fact pricks rudely, that thrice-superfine
Feminity of sense, with right divine
To waive all process, take result stain-free
From out the very muck wherein . . .

                                   Ah me !
The true slave's querulous outbreak ! All the rest
Be resignation ! Forth at your behest
I fare. Who knows but this — the crimson-quest —
May deepen to a sunrise, not decay ·
To that cold sad sweet smile ? — which I obey.

APPEARANCES.

I.

AND so you found that poor room dull,
  Dark, hardly to your taste, my dear?
Its features seemed unbeautiful:
  But this I know — 'twas there, not here,
You plighted troth to me, the word
Which — ask that poor room how it heard.

2.

And this rich room obtains your praise
  Unqualified — so bright, so fair,
So all whereat perfection stays?
  Ay, but remember — here, not there,
The other word was spoken! — Ask
This rich room how you dropped the mask!

ST. MARTIN'S SUMMER.

1.

No protesting, dearest !
 Hardly kisses even !
 .Don't we both know how it ends,
How the greenest leaf turns searest,
 Bluest outbreak — blankest heaven,
 Lovers — friends ?

2.

You would build a mansion,
 I would weave a bower
 — Want the heart for enterprise.
Walls admit of no expansion :
 Trellis-work may haply flower
 Twice the size.

3.

What makes glad Life's Winter?

New buds, old blooms after.

Sad the sighing " How suspect

Beams would ere mid-Autumn splinter,

Rooftree scarce support a rafter,

Walls lie wrecked?"

4.

You are young, my princess !

I am hardly older:

Yet — I steal a glance behind !

Dare I tell you what convinces

Timid me that you, if bolder,

Bold — are blind?

5.

Where we plan our dwelling

Glooms a graveyard surely !

Headstone, footstone moss may drape, —

Name, date, violets hide from spelling, —
But, though corpses rot obscurely,
  Ghosts escape.

6.

Ghosts! O breathing beauty,
  Give my frank word pardon!
  What if I — somehow, somewhere —
Pledged my soul to endless duty
  Many a time and oft? Be hard on
    Love — laid there?

7.

Nay, blame grief that's fickle,
  Time that proves a traitor,
  Chance, change, all that purpose warps, —
Death who spares to thrust the sickle
  Laid Love low, through flowers which later
    Shroud the corpse!

8.

And you, my winsome lady,
  Whisper me with like frankness !
  Lies nothing buried long ago ?
Are yon — which shimmer mid the shady
  Where moss and violet run to rankness —
  Tombs or no ?

9.

Who taxes you with murder ?
  My hands are clean — or nearly !
  Love being mortal needs must pass.
Repentance ? Nothing were absurder.
  Enough : we felt Love's loss severely ;
  Though now — alas !

10.

Love's corpse lies quiet therefore,
  Only Love's ghost plays truant,
  And warns us have in wholesome awe

Durable mansionry; that's wherefore

I weave but trellis-work, pursuant

— Life, to law.

11.

The solid, not the fragile,

Tempts rain and hail and thunder.

If bower stand firm at Autumn's close,

Beyond my hope, — why, boughs were agile;

If bower fall flat, we scarce need wonder

Wreathing — rose!

12.

So, truce to the protesting,

So, muffled be the kisses!

For, would we but avow the truth,

Sober is genuine joy. No jesting!

Ask else Penelope, Ulysses —

Old in youth!

13.

For why should ghosts feel angered?

Let all their interference

Be faint march-music in the air!

"Up! ˙ Join the rear of us the vanguard!

Up, lovers, dead to all appearance,

Laggard pair!"

14.

·The while you clasp me closer,

˙ The while I press you deeper,

As safe we chuckle, — under breath,

Yet all the slyer, the jocoser, —

"So, life can boast its day, like leap-year,

Stolen from death!"

15.

Ah me — the sudden terror!

Hence quick — avaunt, avoid me,

You cheat, the ghostly flesh-disguised!

Nay, all the ghosts in one ! Strange error !
So, 'twas Death's self that clipped and coyed me !
Loved — and lied !

16.

Ay, dead loves are the potent !
Like any cloud they used you,
Mere semblance you, but substance they !
Build we no mansion, weave we no tent !
Mere flesh — their spirit interfused you !
Hence, I say !

17.

All theirs, none yours the glamour !
Theirs each low word that won me,
Soft look that found me Love's, and left
What else but you — the tears and clamor
That's all your very own ! Undone me —
Ghost-bereft !

A FORGIVENESS.

I AM indeed the personage you know.
As for my wife, — what happened long ago —
You have a right to question me, as . I
Am bound to answer.

                    "Son, a fit reply ! "
The   monk   half   spoke,   half   ground   through   his
    clenched teeth,
At the confession-grate I knelt beneath.
    ✦

Thus then all happened, Father !   Power and place
I had as still I have.   I ran life's race,
With the whole world to see, as only strains
His strength some athlete whose prodigious gains
Of good appall him : happy to excess, —
Work freely done should balance happiness

Fully enjoyed; and, since beneath my roof
Housed she who made home heaven, in heaven's
    behoof
I went forth every day, and all day long
Worked for the world. Look, how the laborer's song
Cheers him! Thus sang my soul, at each sharp
    throe
Of laboring flesh and blood — "She loves me so!"

One day, perhaps such song so knit the nerve
That work grew play and vanished. "I deserve
Haply my heaven an hour before the time!"
I laughed, as silverly the clockhouse-chime
Surprised me passing through the postern-gate
— Not the main entry where the menials wait
And wonder why the world's affairs allow
The master sudden leisure. That was how
I took the private garden-way for once.

Forth from the alcove, I saw start, ensconce
Himself behind the porphyry vase, a man.

My fancies in the natural order ran:
" A spy, — perhaps a foe in ambuscade, —
A thief, — more like, a sweetheart of some maid
Who pitched on the alcove for tryst perhaps "

" Stand there ! " I bid.

        Whereat my man but wraps
His face the closelier with uplifted arm
Whereon the cloak lies, strikes in blind alarm
This and that pedestal as, — stretch and stoop, —
Now in, now out of sight, he thrids the group
Of statues, marble god and goddess ranged
Each side the pathway, till the gate's exchanged
For safety: one step thence, the street, you know !

Thus far I followed my gaze. Then, slow,
Near on admiringly, I breathed again,
And — back to that last fancy of the train —
" A danger risked for hope of just a word
With — which of all my nest may be the bird
This poacher covets for her plumage, pray ?

Carmen? Juana? Carmen seems too gay
For such adventure, while Juana's grave
— Would scorn the folly. I applaud the knave!
He had the eye, could single from my brood
His proper fledgling!"

               As I turned, there stood
In face of me, my wife stone-still stone-white.
Whether one bound had brought her, — at first sight
Of what she judged the encounter, sure to be
Next moment, of the venturous man and me, —
Brought her to clutch and keep me from my prey,
Whether impelled because her death no day
Could come so absolutely opportune
As now at joy's height, like a year in June
Stayed at the fall of its first ripened rose ;
Or whether hungry for my hate — who knows ? —
Eager to end an irksome lie, and taste
Our tingling true relation, hate embraced
By hate one naked moment : — anyhow
There stone-still stone-white stood my wife, but now

The woman who made heaven within my house.
Ay, she who faced me was my very spouse
As well as love — you are to recollect !

"Stay ! " she said. "Keep at least one soul unspecked
With crime, that's spotless hitherto — your own !
Kill me who court the blessing, who alone
Was, am and shall be guilty, first to last !
The man lay helpless in the toils I cast
About him, helpless as the statue there
Against that strangling bell-flower's bondage : tear
Away and tread to dust the parasite,
But do the passive marble no despite !
I love him as I hate you. Kill me ! Strike
At one blow both infinitudes alike
Out of existence — hate and love ! Whence love ?
That's safe inside my heart, nor will remove
For any searching of your steel, I think.
Whence hate ? The secret lay on lip, at brink
Of speech, in one fierce tremble to escape,
At every form wherein your love took shape,

At each new provocation of your kiss.
Kill me ! "

We went in.

Next day after this,
I felt as if the speech might come. I spoke —
Easily, after all.

" The lifted cloak
Was screen sufficient: I concern myself
Hardly with laying hands on who for pelf —
Whate'er the ignoble kind — may prowl and brave
Cuffing and kicking proper to a knave
Detected by my household's vigilance.
Enough of such ! As for my love-romance —
I, like our good Hidalgo, rub my eyes
And wake and wonder how the film could rise
Which changed for me a barber's basin straight
Into — Mambrino's helm ? I hesitate
Nowise to say — God's sacramental cup !

Why should I blame the brass which, burnished up,

Will blaze, to all but me, as good as gold?

To me — a warning I was overbold

In judging metals. The Hidalgo waked

Only to die, if I remember, — staked

His life upon the basin's worth, and lost:

While I confess torpidity at most

In here and there a limb; but, lame and halt,

Still should I work on, still repair my fault

Ere I took rest in death, — no fear at all!

Now, work — no word before the curtain fall!"

The "curtain?" That of death on life, I meant:

My "word" permissible in death's event,

Would be — truth, soul to soul; for, otherwise,

Day by day, three years long, there had to rise

And, night by night, to fall upon our stage —

Ours, doomed to public play by heritage —

Another curtain, when the world, perforce

Our critical assembly, in due course

Came and went, witnessing, gave praise or blame

To art-mimetic. It had spoiled the game

If, suffered to set foot behind our scene,
The world had witnessed how stage-king and queen,
Gallant and lady, but a minute since
Enarming each the other, would evince
No sign of recognition as they took
His way and her way to whatever nook
Waited them in the darkness either side
Of that bright stage where lately groom and bride
Had fired the audience to a frenzy-fit
Of sympathetic rapture — every whit
Earned as the curtain fell on her and me,
— Actors.   Three whole years, nothing was to see
But calm and concord: where a speech was due
There came the speech; when smiles were wanted
    too
Smiles were as ready.   In a place like mine,
Where foreign and domestic cares combine,
There's audience every day and all day long;
But finally the last of the whole throng
Who linger lets one see his back.   For her —
Why, liberty and liking: I aver,

Liking and liberty! For me — I breathed,

Let my face rest from every wrinkle wreathed

Smile-like about the mouth, unlearned my task

Of personation till next day bade mask,

And quietly betook me from that world

To the real world, not pageant: there unfurled

In work, its wings, my soul, the fretted power.

Three years I worked, each minute of each hour

Not claimed by acting: — work I may dispense

With talk about, since work in evidence,

Perhaps in history; who knows or cares?

After three years, this way, all unawares,

Our acting ended. She and I, at close

Of a loud night-feast, led, between two rows

Of bending male and female loyalty,

Our lord the king down staircase, while, held high

At arm's length did the twisted tapers' flare

Herald his passage from our palace where

Such visiting left glory evermore.

Again the ascent in public, till at door

As we two stood by the saloon — now blank
And disencumbered of its guests — there sank
A whisper in my ear, so low and yet
So unmistakable !

"I half forget
The chamber you repair to, and I want
Occasion for one short word — if you grant
That grace — within a certain room you called
Our ' *Study*,' for you wrote there while I scrawled
Some paper full of faces for my sport.
That room I can remember. Just one short
Word with you there, for the remembrance' sake ! "

" Follow me thither ! " I replied.

                              We break
The gloom a little, as with guiding lamp
I lead the way, leave warmth and cheer, by damp
Blind disused serpentining ways afar
From where the habitable chambers are, —

Ascend, descend stairs tunnelled through the stone, —

Always in silence, — till I reach the lone

Chamber sepulchred for my very own

Out of the palace-quarry. When a boy,

Here was my fortress, stronghold from annoy,

Proof-positive of ownership ; in youth

I garnered up my gleanings here — uncouth

But precious relics of vain hopes, vain fears ;

Finally, this became in after years

My closet of intrenchment to withstand

Invasion of the foe on every hand —

The multifarious herd in bower and hall,

State-room, — rooms whatsoe'er the style, which call

On masters to be mindful that, before

Men, they must look like men and something more.

Here, — when our lord the king's bestowment ceased

To deck me on the day that, golden-fleeced,

I touched ambition's height, — 'twas here, released

From glory (always symbolled by a chain !)

No sooner was I privileged to gain

My secret domicile than glad I flung

That last toy on the table — gazed where hung
On hook my father's gift, the arquebuss —
And asked myself " Shall I envisage thus
The new prize and the old prize, when I reach
Another year's experience? — own that each
Equalled advantage — sportsman's — statesman's tool?
That brought me down an eagle, this — a fool ! "

Into which room on entry, I set down
The lamp, and turning saw whose rustled gown
Had told me my wife followed, pace for pace.
Each of us looked the other in the face,
She spoke. " Since I could die now . . ."

                         (To explain
Why that first struck me, know — not once again
Since the adventure at the porphyry's edge
Three years before, which sundered like a wedge
Her soul from mine, — though daily, smile to smile,
We stood before the public, — all the while
Not once had I distinguished, in that face

I paid observance to, the faintest trace
Of feature more than requisite for eyes
To do their duty by and recognize :
So did I force mine to obey my will
And pry no further. There exists such skill, —
Those know who need it. What physician shrinks
From needful contact with a corpse? He drinks
No plague so long as thirst for knowledge, — not
An idler impulse, — prompts inquiry. What,
And will you disbelieve in power to bid
Our spirit back to bounds, as though we chid
A child from scrutiny that's just and right
In manhood? Sense, not soul, accomplished sight,
Reported daily she it was — not how   .
Nor why a change had come to cheek and brow.)
                         .

" Since I could die now of the truth concealed,
Yet dare not, must not die, — so seems revealed
The Virgin's mind to me, — for death means peace,
Wherein no lawful part have I, whose lease
Of life and punishment the truth avowed

May haply lengthen, — let me push the shroud
Away, that steals to muffle ere is just
My penance-fire in snow ! I dare — I must
Live, by avowal of the truth — this truth —
I loved you ! Thanks for the fresh serpent's tooth
That, by a prompt new pang more exquisite
Than all preceding torture, proves me right !
I loved you yet I lost you ! May I go
Burn to the ashes, now my shame you know ? "

I think there never was such — how express ? —
Horror coquetting with voluptuousness,
As in those arms of Eastern workmanship —
Yataghan, kandjar, things that rend and rip,
Gash rough, slash smooth, help hate so many ways,
Yet ever keep a beauty that betrays
Love still at work with the artificer
Throughout his quaint devising. Why prefer,
Except for love's sake, that a blade should writhe
And bicker like a flame ? — now play the scythe
As if some broad neck tempted, — now contract

And needle off into a fineness lacked

For just that puncture which the heart demands?

Then, such adornment! Wherefore need our hands

Enclose not ivory alone, nor gold

Roughened for use, but jewels? Nay, behold!

Fancy my favorite — which I seem to grasp

While I describe the luxury. No asp

Is diapered more delicate round throat

Than this below the handle! These denote

— These mazy lines meandering, to end

Only in flesh they open — what intend

They else but water-purlings — pale contrast

With the life-crimson where they blend at last?

And mark the handle's dim pellucid green,

Carved, the hard jadestone, as you pinch a bean,

Into a sort of parrot-bird! He pecks

A grape-bunch ; his two eyes are ruby-specks

Pure from the mine : seen this way, — glassy blank,

But turn them, — lo the inmost fire, that shrank

From sparkling, sends a red dart right to aim!

Why did I choose such toys? Perhaps the game

Of peaceful men is warlike, just as men
War-wearied get amusement from that pen
And paper we grow sick of — statesfolk tired
Of merely (when such measures are required)
Dealing out doom to people by three words,
A signature and seal: we play with swords
Suggestive of quick process. That is how
I came to like the toys described you now,
Store of which glittered on the walls and strewed
The table, even, while my wife pursued
Her purpose to its ending. " Now you know
This shame, my three years' torture, let me go,
Burn to the very ashes! You — I lost,
Yet you — I loved! "

                    The thing I pity most
In men is — action prompted by surprise
Of anger: men? nay, bulls — whose onset lies
At instance of the firework and the goad!
Once the foe prostrate, — trampling once bestowed, —
Prompt follows placability, regret,

Atonement. Trust me, blood-warmth never yet
Betokened strong will ! As no leap of pulse
Pricked me, that first time, so did none convulse
My veins at this occasion for resolve.
Had that devolved which did not then devolve
Upon me, I had done — what now to do
Was quietly apparent.

                                        "Tell me who
The man was, crouching by the porphyry vase ! "
" No, never ! All was folly in his case,
All guilt in mine. I tempted, he complied."

" And yet you loved me ? "

                                        " Loved you. Double-dyed
In folly and in guilt, I thought you gave
Your heart and soul away from me to slave
At statecraft. Since my right in you seemed lost,
I stung myself to teach you, to your cost,
What you rejected could be prized beyond

Life, heaven, by the first fool I threw a fond
Look on, a fatal word to."

                    "And you still
Love me? Do I conjecture well or ill?"
"Conjecture — well or ill! I had three years
To spend in learning you."

                    "We both are peers
In knowledge, therefore: since three years are spent
Ere thus much of yourself *I* learn — who went
Back to the house, that day, and brought my mind
To bear upon your action, uncombined
Motive from motive, till the dross, deprived
Of every purer particle, survived
At last in native simple hideousness,
Utter contemptibility, nor less
Nor more. Contemptibility — exempt
How could I, from its proper due — contempt?
I have too much despised you to divert
My life from its set course by help or hurt

Of your all-despicable life — perturb

The calm I work in, by — men's mouth to curb,

Which at such news were clamorous enough —

Men's eyes to shut before my broidered stuff

With the huge hole there, my emblazoned wall

Blank where a scutcheon hung, — by, worse than all,

Each day's procession, my paraded life

Robbed and impoverished through the wanting wife

— Now that my life (which means — my work) was
        grown

Riches indeed!   Once, just this worth alone

Seemed work to have, that profit gained thereby

Of good and praise would — how rewardingly ! —

Fall at your feet, — a crown I hoped to cast

Before your love, my love should crown at last.

No love remaining to cast crown before,

My love stopped work now : but contempt the more

Impelled me task as ever head and hand,

Because the very fiends weave ropes of sand

Rather than taste pure hell in idleness.

Therefore I kept my memory down by stress

Of daily work I had no mind to stay
For the world's wonder at the wife away.
Oh, it was easy all of it, believe,
For I despised you! But your words retrieve
Importantly the past. No hate assumed
The mask of love at any time! There gloomed
A moment when love took hate's semblance, urged
By causes you declare; but love's self purged
Away a fancied wrong I did both loves
— Yours and my own : by no hate's help, it proves,
Purgation was attempted. Then, you rise
High by how many a grade! I did despise —
I do but hate you. Let hate's punishment
Replace contempt's! First step to which ascent —
Write down your own words I re-utter you!
'*I loved my husband and I hated — who*
He was, I took up as my first chance, mere
Mud-ball to fling and make love foul with!' Here
Lies paper!"

"Would my blood for ink suffice!"

"It may : this minion from a land of spice,
Silk, feather — every bird of jewelled breast —
This poniard's beauty, ne'er so lightly prest
Above your heart there . ."

"Thus?"

"It flows, I see.
Dip there the point and write!"

"Dictate to me!
Nay, I remember."
And she wrote the words.
I read them.   Then — "Since love, in you, affords
License for hate, in me, to quench (I say)
Contempt — why, hate itself has passed away
In vengeance — foreign to contempt.   Depart
Peacefully to that death which Eastern art
Imbued this weapon with, if tales be true !
Love will succeed to hate.   I pardon you —
Dead in our chamber ! "

True as truth the tale.
She died ere morning; then, I saw how pale
Her cheek was ere it wore day's paint-disguise,
And what a hollow darkened 'neath her eyes,
Now that I used my own. She sleeps, as erst
Beloved, in this your church: ay, yours!

Immersed
In thought so deeply, Father? Sad, perhaps?
For whose sake, hers or mine or his who wraps
— Still plain I seem to see!— about his head
The idle cloak, — about his heart (instead
Of cuirass) some fond hope he may elude
My vengeance in the cloister's solitude?
Hardly, I think! As little helped his brow
The cloak then, Father — as your grate helps now!

.

CENCIAJA.

Ogni cencio vuol entrare in bucato. — *Italian Proverb.*

MAY I print, Shelley, how it came to pass
That when your Beatrice seemed — by lapse
Of many a long month since her sentence fell —
Assured of pardon for the parricide, —
By intercession of stanch friends, or, say,
By certain pricks of conscience in the Pope
Conniver at Francesco Cenci's guilt, —
Suddenly all things changed and Clement grew
" Stern," as you state, " nor to be moved nor bent,
But said these three words coldly ' *She must die;* '
Subjoining ' *Pardon ?   Paolo Santa Croce*
Murdered his mother also yestereve,
And he is fled: she shall not flee at least ! '
— So, to the letter, sentence was fulfilled?

Shelley, may I condense verbosity
That lies before me, into some few words
Of English, and illustrate your superb
Achievement by a rescued anecdote,
No great things, only new and true beside?
As if some mere familiar of a house
Should venture to accost the group at gaze
Before its Titian, famed the wide world through,
And supplement such pictured masterpiece
By whisper " Searching in the archives here,
I found the reason of the Lady's fate,
And how by accident it came to pass
She wears the halo and displays the palm:
Who, haply, else had never suffered — no,
Nor graced our gallery, by consequence."
Who loved the work would like the little news
Who lauds your poem lends an ear to me
Relating how the penalty was paid
By one Marchese dell' Oriolo, called
Onofrio Santa Croce otherwise,
For his complicity in matricide

With Paolo his own brother, — he whose crime
And flight induced "those three words — She must
  die."
Thus I unroll you then the manuscript.

"God's justice" — (of the multiplicity
Of such communications extant still,
Recording, each, injustice done by God
In person of his Vicar-upon-earth,
Scarce one but leads off to the self-same tune) —
"God's justice, tardy though it prove perchance,
Rests never on the track until it reach
Delinquency. In proof I cite the case
Of Paolo Santa Croce."

                        Many times
The youngster, — having been importunate
That Marchesine Costanza, who remained
His widowed mother, should supplant the heir
Her elder son, and substitute himself
In sole possession of her faculty, —

And meeting just as often with rebuff,—
Blinded by so exorbitant a lust
Of gold, the youngster straightway tasked his wits,
Casting about to kill the lady — thus.

He first, to cover his iniquity,
Writes to Onofrio Santa Croce, then
Authoritative lord, acquainting him
Their mother was contamination — wrought
Like hell-fire in the beauty of their House
By dissoluteness and abandonment
Of soul and body to impure delight.
Moreover, since she suffered from disease,
Those symptoms which her death made manifest
Hydroptic, he affirmed were fruits of sin
About to bring confusion and disgrace
Upon the ancient lineage and high fame
O' the family, when published. Duty bound,
He asked his brother — what a son should do?

Which when Marchese dell' Oriolo heard

By letter, being absent at his land
Oriolo, he made answer, this, no more
"It must behoove a son, — things haply so, —
To act as honor prompts a cavalier
And son, perform his duty to all three,
Mother and brothers " — here advice broke off.

By which advice informed and fortified
As he professed himself — the bound by birth
To hear God's voice in primogeniture —
Paolo, who kept his mother company
In her domain Subiaco, straightway dared
His whole enormity of enterprise
And, falling on her, stabbed the lady dead ;
Whose death demonstrated her innocence,
And happened, — by the way, — since Jesus Christ
Died to save man, just sixteen hundred years.
Costanza was of aspect beautiful
Exceedingly, and seemed, although in age
Sixty about, to far surpass her peers
The coëtaneous dames, in youth and grace.

* Done the misdeed, its author takes to flight,
Foiling thereby the justice of the world :
Not God's however, — God, be sure, knows well
The way to clutch a culprit. Witness here!
The present sinner, when he least expects,
Snug-cornered somewhere i' the Basilicate,
Stumbles upon his death by violence.
A man of blood assaults the man of blood
And slays him somehow. This was afterward :
Enough, he promptly met with his deserts,
And, ending thus, permits we end with him,
And push forthwith to this important point —
His matricide fell out, of all the days,
Precisely when the law-procedure closed
Respecting Count Francesco Cenci's death
Chargeable on his daughter, sons and wife.
" Thus patricide was matched with matricide,"
A poet not inelegantly rhymed :
Nay, fratricide — those Princes Massimi ! —
Which so disturbed the spirit of the Pope
That all the likelihood Rome entertained

Of Beatrice's pardon vanished straight,
And she endured the piteous death.

                                        Now see
The sequel — what effect commandment had
For strict inquiry into this last case,
When Cardinal Aldobrandini (great
His efficacy — nephew to the Pope!)
Was bidden crush — ay, though his very hand
Got soil i' the act — crime spawning everywhere!
Because, when all endeavor had been used
To catch the aforesaid Paolo, all in vain —
"Make perquisition" quoth our Eminence,
"Throughout his now deserted domicile!
Ransack the palace, roof and floor, to find
If haply any scrap of writing, hid
In nook or corner, may convict — who knows? —
Brother Onofrio of intelligence
With brother Paolo, as in brotherhood
Is but too likely: crime spawns everywhere!"

And, every cranny searched accordingly,
There comes to light — O lynx-eyed Cardinal ! —
Onofrio's unconsidered writing-scrap,
The letter in reply to Paolo's prayer,
The word of counsel that — things proving so,
Paolo should act the proper knightly part,
And do as was incumbent on a son,
A brother — and a man of birth, be sure !

Whereat immediately the officers
Proceeded to arrest Onofrio — found
At foot-ball, child's play, unaware of harm,
Safe with his friends, the Orsini, at their seat
Monte Giordano ; as he left the house ·
He came upon the watch in wait for him
Set by the Barigel, — was caught and caged.

News of which capture being, that same hour,
Conveyed to Rome, forthwith our Eminence
Commands Taverna, Governor and Judge,
To have the process in especial care,

Be, first to last, not only president
In person, but inquisitor as well,
Nor trust the by-work to a substitute :
Bids him not, squeamish, keep the bench, but scrub
The floor of Justice, so to speak, — go try
His best in prison with the criminal ;
Promising, as reward for by-work done
Fairly on all-fours, that, success obtained
And crime avowed, or such connivancy
With crime as should procure a decent death —
Himself will humbly beg — which means, procure —
The Hat and Purple from his relative
The Pope, and so repay a diligence
Which, meritorious in the Cenci-case,
Mounts plainly here to Purple and the Hat !

Whereupon did my lord the Governor
So masterfully exercise the task
Enjoined him, that he, day by day, and week
By week, and month by month, from first to last
Deserved the prize : now, punctual at his place,

Played Judge, and now, assiduous at his post,

Inquisitor — pressed cushion and scoured plank,

Early and late. Noon's fervor and night's chill,

Nought moved whom morn would, purpling, make
    amends !

So that observers laughed as, many a day,

He left home, in July when day is flame,

Posted to Tordinona-prison, plunged

Into the vault where daylong night is ice,

There passed his eight hours on a stretch, content,

Examining Onofrio : all the stress

Of all examination steadily

Converging into one pin-point, — he pushed

Tentative now of head and now of heart.

As when the nuthatch taps and tries the nut

This side and that side till the kernel sound, —

So did he press the sole and single point

— What was the very meaning of the phrase

'Do what beseems an honored cavalier ?'

Which one persistent question-torture, — plied

Day by day, week by week, and month by month,

Morn, noon and night, — fatigued away a mind

Grown imbecile by darkness, solitude,

And one vivacious memory gnawing there

As when a corpse is coffined with a snake :

— Fatigued Onofrio into what might seem

Admission that perchance his judgment groped

So blindly, feeling for an issue — aught

With semblance of an issue from the toils

Cast of a sudden round feet late so free,

He possibly might have envisaged, scarce

Recoiled from — even were the issue death

— Even her death whose life was death and worse !

Always provided that the charge of crime,

Each jot and tittle of the charge were true.

In such a sense, belike, he might advise

His brother to expurgate crime with . . well,

With blood, if blood must follow on '*the course*

Taken as might beseem a cavalier.'

Whereupon process ended, and report

Was made without a minute of delay
To Clement who, because of those two crimes
O' the Massimi and Cenci flagrant late,
Must needs impatiently desire result.

Result obtained, he bade the Governor
Summon the Congregation and despatch.
Summons made, sentence passed accordingly
— Death by beheading. When his death-decree
Was intimated to Onofrio, all
Man could do — that did he to save himself.
'Twas much, the having gained for his defence
The Advocate o' the Poor, with natural help
Of many noble friendly persons fain
To disengage a man of family,
So young too, from his grim entanglement.
But Cardinal Aldobrandini ruled
There must be no diversion of the law.
Justice is justice, and the magistrate
Bears not the sword in vain. Who sins must die.

So, the Marchese had his head cut off
In Place Saint Angelo beside the Bridge,
With Rome to see, a concourse infinite ;
Where, demonstrating magnanimity
Adequate to his birth and breed, — poor boy ! —
He made the people the accustomed speech,
Exhorted them to true faith, honest works,
And special good behavior as regards
A parent of no matter what the sex,
Bidding each son take warning from himself.
Truly, it was considered in the boy
Stark staring lunacy, no less, to snap
So plain a bait, be hooked and hauled a-shore
By such an angler as the Cardinal !
Why make confession of his privity
To Paolo's enterprise ?   Mere sealing lips —
Or, better, saying " When I counselled him
' *To do as might beseem a cavalier,*'
What could I mean but ' *Hide our parent's shame*
As Christian ought, by aid of Holy Church !
Bury it in a convent — ay, beneath

Enough dotation to prevent its ghost
From troubling earth!'" Mere saying thus, — 'tis
    plain,
Not only were his life the recompense,
But he had manifestly proved himself
True Christian, and in lieu of punishment
Been praised of all men ! — So the populace.

Anyhow, when the Pope made promise good
(That of Aldobrandini, near and dear)
And gave Taverna, who had toiled so much,
A Cardinal's equipment, some such word
As this from mouth to ear went saucily:
" Taverna's cap is dyed in what he drew
From Santa Croce's veins !" So joked the world.

I add : Onofrio left one child behind,
A daughter named Valeria, dowered with grace
Abundantly of soul and body, doomed
To life the shorter for her father's fate.
By death of her, the Marquisate returned

To that Orsini House from whence it came:
Oriolo having passed as donative
To Santa Croce from their ancestors.

And no word more? By all means! Would you
    know
The authoritative answer, when folks urged
"What made Aldobrandini, hound-like stanch,
Hunt out of life a harmless simpleton?"
The answer was — "Hatred implacable,
By reason they were rivals in their love."
The Cardinal's desire was to a dame
Whose favor was Onofrio's. Pricked with pride,
The simpleton must ostentatiously
Display a ring, the Cardinal's love-gift,
Given to Onofrio as the lady's gage;
Which ring on finger, as he put forth hand
To draw a tapestry, the Cardinal
Saw and knew, gift and owner, old and young;
Whereon a fury entered him — the fire
He quenched with what could quench fire only —
    blood.

Nay, more : "there want not who affirm to boot,
The unwise boy, a certain festal eve,
Feigned ignorance of who the wight might be
That pressed too closely on him with a crowd,
And struck the Cardinal a blow : and then,
To put a face upon the incident,
Dared next day, smug as ever, go pay court
I' the Cardinal's antechamber. Mark and mend,
Ye youth, by this example how may greed
Vainglorious operate in worldly souls ! "

So ends the chronicler, beginning with
" God's justice, tardy though it prove perchance,
Rests never till it reach delinquency."
Ay, or how otherwise had come to pass
That Victor rules this present year, in Rome ?

FILIPPO BALDINUCCI ON THE PRIVILEGE OF BURIAL.

A Reminiscence of A.D. 1676.

1.

"No, boy, we must not" — so began
My Uncle (he's with God long since)
A-petting me, the good old man!
"We must not" — and he seemed to wince,
And lost that laugh whereto had grown
His chuckle at my piece of news,
How cleverly I aimed my stone —
"I fear we must not pelt the Jews!

2.

"When I was young indeed, — ah, faith
Was young and strong in Florence too!
We Christians never dreamed of scathe
Because we cursed or kicked the crew.

But now — well, well ! The olive-crops
  Weighed double then, and Arno's pranks
Would always spare religious shops
  Whenever he o'erflowed his banks !

3.

" I'll tell you " — and his eye regained
  Its twinkle — " tell you something choice !
Something may help you keep unstained
  Your honest zeal to stop the voice
Of unbelief with stone-throw — spite
  Of laws, which modern fools enact,
That we must suffer Jews in sight
  Go wholly unmolested ! Fact !
    .

4.

" There was, then, in my youth, and yet
  Is, by San Frediano, just
Below the Blessed Olivet,
  A wayside ground wherein they thrust

Their dead, — these Jews, — the more our shame
    Except that, so they will but die,
We may perchance incur no blame
    In giving hogs a hoist to sty.

5.

"There, anyhow, Jews stow away
    Their dead ; and, — such their insolence, —
Slink at odd times to ·sing and pray
    As Christians do — all make-pretence ! —
Which wickedness they perpetrate
    Because they think no Christians see.
They reckoned here, at any rate,
    Without their host : ha, ha, he, he !

6.

"For, what should join their plot of ground
    But a good Farmer's Christian field ?
The Jews had hedged their corner round
    With bramble-bush to keep concealed

Their doings : for the public road
Ran betwixt this their ground and that
The Farmer's, where he ploughed and sowed,
Grew corn for barn and grapes for vat.

7.

" So, properly to guard his store
And gall the unbelievers too,
He builds a shrine and, what is more,
Procures a painter whom I knew,
One Buti (he's with God) to paint
A holy picture there — no less
Than Virgin Mary free from taint
Borne to the sky by angels : yes !

8.

" Which shrine he fixed, — who says him nay ? —
A-facing with its picture-side
Not, as you'd think, the public way,
But just where sought these hounds to hide

Their carrion from that very truth

Of Mary's triumph : not a hound

Could act his mummeries uncouth

But Mary shamed the pack all round !

9.

" Now, if it was amusing, judge !

— To see the company arrive,

Each Jew intent to end his trudge

And take his pleasure (though alive)

With all his Jewish kith and kin

Below ground, have his venom out,

Sharpen his wits for next day's sin,

Curse Christians, and so home, no doubt !

10.

" Whereas, each phiz upturned beholds

Mary, I warrant, soaring brave !

And in a trice, beneath the folds

Of filthy garb which gowns each knave,

Down drops it — there to hide grimace,
   Contortion of the mouth and nose
At finding Mary in the place
   They'd keep for Pilate, I suppose!

11.

"At last, they will not brook — not they! —
   Longer such outrage on their tribe :
So, in some hole and corner, lay
   Their heads together — how to bribe
The meritorious Farmer's self
   To straight undo his work, restore
Their chance to meet, and muse on pelf —
   Pretending sorrow, as before!

12.

" Forthwith, a posse, if you please,
   Of Rabbi This and Rabbi That
Almost go down upon their knees
   To get him lay the picture flat.

The spokesman, eighty years of age,
  Gray as a badger, with a goat's
— Not only beard but bleat, 'gins wage
  War with our Mary. Thus he dotes : —

13.

" '*Friends, grant a grace ! How Hebrews toil*
  Through life in Florence — *why relate*
To those who lay the burden, spoil
  Our paths of peace ? We bear our fate.
But when with life the long toil ends,
  Why must you — *the expression craves*
Pardon, but truth compels me, friends ! —
  Why must you plague us in our graves ?

14.

" '*Thoughtlessly plague, I would believe !*
  For how can you — *the lords of ease*
By nurture, birthright — *e'en conceive*
  Our luxury to lie with trees

And turf, — the cricket and the bird
  Left for our last companionship :
No harsh deed, no unkindly word,
  No frowning brow nor scornful lip !

15.

" ' *Death's luxury, we now rehearse*
  While, living, through your streets we fare
And take your hatred : nothing worse
  Have we, once dead and safe, to bear !
So we refresh our souls, fulfil
  Our works, our daily tasks ; and thus
Gather you grain — earth's harvest — still
  The wheat for you, the straw for us.

16.

" ' 'What flouting in a face, what. harm,
  In just a lady borne aloft
By boys' heads, wings for leg and arm ? '
  You question. Friends, the harm is here —

That just when our last sigh is heaved,
And we would fain thank God and you
For labor done and peace achieved,
    Back comes the Past in full review !

17.

"'At sight of just that simple flag,
    Starts the foe-feeling serpent-like
From slumber.   Leave it lulled, nor drag —
    Though fangless — forth, what needs must strike
When stricken sore, though stroke be vain
    Against the mailed oppressor !   Give
Play to our fancy that we gain
    Life's rights when once we cease to live !

18.

" ' Thus much to courtesy, to kind,
    To conscience !   Now to Florence folk !
There's core beneath this apple-rind,
    Beneath this white-of-egg there's yolk !

Beneath this prayer to courtesy,
  Kind, conscience — there's a sum to pouch !
How many ducats down will buy
  Our shame's removal, sirs ? Avouch !

19.

" ' Removal, not destruction, sirs !
  Just turn your picture ! Let it front
The public path ! Or memory errs,
  Or that same public path is wont
To witness many a chance befall
  Of lust, theft, bloodshed — sins enough,
Wherein our Hebrew part is small.
  Convert yourselves ! ' —he cut up rough.

20.

"Look you, how soon a service paid
  Religion yields the servant fruit !
A prompt reply our Farmer made
  So following : *' Sirs, to grant your suit*

Involves much danger !   How ?   Transpose

Our Lady ?   Stop the chastisement,

All for your good, herself bestows ?

What wonder if I grudge consent ?

21.

" ' — *Yet grant it : since, what cash I take*

Is so much saved from wicked use.

We know you !   And, for Mary's sake,

A hundred ducats shall induce

Concession to your prayer.   One day

Suffices : Master Buti's brush

Turns Mary round the other way,

And deluges your side with slush.

22.

" ' *Down with the ducats therefore ! '* Dump,

Dump, dump it falls, each counted piece,

Hard gold.   Then out of door they stump,

These dogs, each brisk as with new lease

Of life, I warrant, — glad he'll die
Henceforward just as he may choose,
Be buried and in clover lie!
Well said Esaias — '*stiff-necked Jews!*'

23.

"Off posts without a minute's loss
Our Farmer, once the cash in poke,
And summons Buti — ere its gloss
Have time to fade from off the joke —
To chop and change his work, undo
The done side, make the side, now blank,
Recipient of our Lady — who,
Displaced thus, had these dogs to thank!

24.

"Now, boy, you're hardly to instruct
In technicalities of Art!
My nephew's childhood sure has sucked
Along with mother's-milk some part

Of painter's-practice — learned, at least,
How expeditiously is plied
A work in fresco — never ceased
When once begun — a day, each side

25.

"So, Buti — (he's with God) — begins :
First covers up the shrine all round
With hoarding ; then, as like as twins,
Paints, t'other side the burial-ground,
New Mary, every point the same ;
Next, sluices over, as agreed,
The old ; and last — but, spoil the game
By telling you ? Not I, indeed !

26.

"Well, ere the week was half at end,
Out came the object of this zeal,
This fine alacrity to spend
Hard money for mere dead men's weal!

How think you ?   That old spokesman Jew
Was High Priest, and he had a wife
As old, and she was dying too,   .
And wished to end in peace her life !

27.

" And he must humor dying whims,
And soothe her with the idle hope
They'd say their prayers and sing their hymns
As if her husband were the Pope !
And she did die — believing just
This privilege was purchased !   Dead
In comfort through her foolish trust !
' *Stiff-necked ones,*' well Esaias said !

28.

" So, Sabbath morning, out of gate
And on to way, what sees our arch
Good Farmer ?   Why, they hoist their freight —
The corpse — on shoulder, and so, march !

'*Now for it, Buti !*' In the nick
Of time 'tis pully-hauly, hence
With hoarding! O'er the wayside quick
There's Mary plain in evidence!

29.

"And here's the convoy halting: right!
O they are bent on howling psalms
And growling prayers, when opposite!
     And yet they glance, for all their qualms,
     Approve that promptitude of his,
The Farmer's — duly at his post
To take due thanks from every phiz,
     Sour smirk — nay, surly smile almost!

30.

"Then earthward drops each brow again;
     The solemn task's resumed; they reach
Their holy field — the unholy train:
     Enter its precinct, all and each,

Wrapt somehow in their godless rites ;
Till, rites at end, up-waking, lo
They lift their faces ! What delights
The mourners as they turn to go ?

31.

" Ha, ha, he, he ! On just the side
They drew. their purse-strings to make quit
Of Mary, — Christ the Crucified
Fronted them now — these biters bit !
Never was such a hiss and snort,
Such screwing nose and shooting lip !
Their purchase — honey in report —
Proved gall and verjuice at first sip !

32.

" Out they break, on they bustle, where,
A-top of wall, the Farmer waits
With Buti : never fun so rare !
The Farmer has the best : he rates

The rascal, as the old High Priest
Takes on himself to sermonize —
Nay, sneer, ' *We Jews supposed, at least,*
Theft was a crime in Christian eyes ! '

33.

" ' *Theft ?* ' cries the Farmer, ' *Eat your words !*
Show me what constitutes a breach
Of faith in aught was said or heard !
I promised you in plainest speech
I'd take the thing you count disgrace
And put it here — and here 'tis put !
Did you suppose I'd leave the place
Blank therefore, just your rage to glut ?

34.

" ' *I guess you dared not stipulate*
For such a damned impertinence !
So, quick, my graybeard, out of gate
And in at Ghetto ! Haste you hence !

As long as I have house and land,
   To spite you irreligious chaps
Here shall the Crucifixion stand —
   Unless you down with cash, perhaps !'

35.

" So snickered he and Buti both.
   The Jews said nothing, interchanged
A glance or two, renewed their oath
   To keep ears stopped and hearts estranged
From grace, for all our Church can do ;
   Then off they scuttle : sullen jog
Homewards, against our Church to brew
   Fresh mischief in their synagogue.

36.

" But next day — see what happened, boy !
   See why I bid you have a care
How you pelt Jews ! The knaves employ
   Such methods of revenge, forbear

No outrage on our faith, when free
To wreak their malice ! Here they took
So base a method — plague o' me
If I record it in my Book !

37·

" For, next day, while the Farmer sat
Laughing, with Buti in his shop,
At their successful joke, — rat-tat, —
Door opens, and they're like to drop
Down to the floor as in there stalks
A six-feet-high herculean-built
Young he-Jew with a beard that balks
Description. ' *Help ere blood be spilt !* '

38.

— " Screamed Buti: for he recognized
Whom but the son, no less no more,
Of that High Priest his work surprised
So pleasantly the day before !

Son of the mother, then, whereof
The bier he lent a shoulder to,
And made the moans about, dared scoff
At sober Christian grief — the Jew !

39.

" ' *Sirs, I salute you ! Never rise !*
No apprehension ! ' (Buti, white
And trembling like a tub of size,
Had tried to smuggle out of sight
The picture's self — the thing in oils,
You know, from which a fresco's dashed
Which courage speeds while caution spoils)
' *Stay and be praised, sir, unabashed !*

40.

" ' *Praised, — ay, and paid too : for I come*
To buy that very work of yours.
My poor abode, which boasts — well, some
Few specimens of Art, secures

Haply, a masterpiece indeed
If I should find my humble means
Suffice the outlay.   So, proceed!
Propose—ere prudence intervenes!'

41.

"On Buti, cowering like a child,
    These words descended from aloft,
In tones so ominously mild,
    With smile terrifically soft
To that degree — could Buti dare
    (Poor fellow) use his brains, think twice?
He asked, thus taken unaware,
    No more than just the proper price!

42.

"'*Done!*' cries the monster.   '*I disburse*
    Forthwith your moderate demand.
Count on my custom — if no worse
    Your future work be, understand,

Than this I carry off! No aid!
My arm, sir, lacks nor bone nor thews:
The burden's easy, and we're made,
Easy or hard, to bear — we Jews!'

43.

"Crossing himself at such escape,
  Buti by turns the money eyes
And, timidly, the stalwart shape
  Now moving doorwards ; but, more wise,
The Farmer, — who, though dumb, this while
  Had watched advantage, — straight conceived
A reason for that tone and smile
  So mild and soft ! The Jew — believed !

44.

"Mary in triumph borne to deck
  A Hebrew household ! Pictured where
No one was used to bend the neck
  In praise or bow the knee in prayer !

Borne to that domicile by whom ?

The son of the High Priest! Through what?

An insult done his mother's tomb !

Saul changed to Paul — the case came pat !

45.

" 'Stay, dog-Jew . . gentle sir, that is !

Resolve me ! Can it be, she crowns, —

Mary, by miracle, — Oh bliss ! —

My present to your burial-ground ?

Certain, a ray of light has burst

Your veil of darkness ! Had you else,

Only for Mary's sake, disbursed

So much hard money ? Tell — oh, tell's ! '

46.

" Round — like a serpent that we took

For worm and trod on — turns his bulk

About the Jew. First dreadful look

Sends Buti in a trice to skulk

Out of sight somewhere, save — alack !

But our good Farmer faith made bold :

And firm (with Florence at his back)

He stood, while gruff the gutturals rolled —

47.

" ' *Ay, sir, a miracle was worked*

By quite another power, I trow,

Than ever yet in canvas lurked,

Or you would scarcely face me now !

A certain impulse did suggest

A certain grasp with this right-hand,

Which probably had put to rest

Our quarrel, — thus your throat once spanned !

48.

" ' *But I remembered me, subdued*

That impulse, and you face me still !

And soon a philosophic mood

Succeeding (hear it, if you will !)

Has altogether changed my views
Concerning Art.   Blind prejudice!
Well may you Christians tax us Jews
With scrupulosity too nice!

.   49.

" ' *For, don't I see, — let's issue join !—*
Whenever I'm allowed pollute
(I — and my little bag of coin)
Some Christian palace of repute,—
Don't I see stuck up everywhere
Abundant proof that cultured taste
Has Beauty for its only care,
And upon Truth no thought to waste ?

.

50.

" ' " Jew, since it must be, take in pledge
Of payment " — *so a Cardinal*
Has sighed to me as if a wedge
Entered his heart " this best of all

My treasures !" *Leda, Ganymede*
  Or Antiope :. swan, eagle, ape,
(Or what's the beast of what's the breed)
And Jupiter in every shape !

51.

"' *Whereat if I presume to ask,*
  " But, Eminence, though Titian's whisk
Of brush have well performed its task,
  How comes it these false godships frisk
In presence of — what yonder frame
  Pretends to image ?   Surely, odd
It seems, you let confront The Name
  Each beast the heathen called his god !"

52.

"' *Benignant smiles me pity straight*
  The Cardinal.   " 'Tis Truth, we prize !
Art's the sole question in debate !
  These subjects are so many lies.

We treat them with a proper scorn

When we turn lies — called gods forsooth —

To lies' fit use, now Christ is born.

Drawing and coloring are Truth.

53.

" ' "Think you I honor lies so much

As scruple to parade the charms

Of Leda — Titian, every touch —

Because the thing within her arms

Means Jupiter who had the praise

And prayer of a benighted world?

He would have mine too, if, in days

Of light, I kept the canvas furled!"

54.

" ' *So ending, with some easy gibe.*

What power has logic! I, at once,

Acknowledged error in our tribe

So squeamish that, when friends ensconce

A pretty picture in its niche

To do us honor, deck our graves,

We fret and fume and have an itch

To strangle folk — ungrateful knaves !

55.

" ' No, sir ! Be sure that — what's its style,

Your picture ? — shall possess ungrudged

A place among my rank and file

Of Ledas and what not — be judged

Just as a picture ! and (because

I fear me much I scarce have bought

A Titian) Master Buti's flaws

Found there, will have the laugh flaws ought !'

56.

" So, with a scowl, it darkens door —

This bulk — no longer ! Buti makes

Prompt glad re-entry ; there's a score

Of oaths, as the good Farmer wakes

From what must needs have been a trance,
   Or he had struck (he swears) to ground
The bold bad mouth that dared advance
   Such doctrine the reverse of sound !

57.

"Was magic here ?   Most like !   For, since,
   Somehow our city's faith grows still
More and more lukewarm, and our Prince
   Or loses heart or wants the will
To check increase of cold.   'Tis ' *Live*
   And let live !   Languidly repress
The Dissident !   In short — contrive
   Christians must bear with Jews : no less !'

58.

" The end seems, any Israelite
   Wants any picture, — pishes, poohs,
Purchases, hangs it full in sight
   In any chamber he may choose !

In Christ's crown, one more thorn we rue!

In Mary's bosom, one more sword!

No, boy, you must not pelt a Jew!

O Lord, how long? How long, O Lord?"

EPILOGUE.

μεστοὶ . . .
οἱ δ᾽ ἀμφορῆς οἴνου μέλανος ἀνθοσμίου.

I.

" The poets pour us wine — "
Said the dearest poet I ever knew,
Dearest and greatest and best to me.
You clamor athirst for poetry —
We pour. " But when shall a vintage be " —
You cry — " strong grape, squeezed gold from
    screw,
Yet sweet juice, flavored flowery-fine ?
That were indeed the wine ! "

2.

One pours your cup — stark strength,
    Meat for a man ; and you eye the pulp
Strained, turbid still, from the viscous blood
Of the snaky bough : and you grumble " Good !

For it swells resolve, breeds hardihood;
Despatch it, then, in a single gulp!"
So, down, with a wry face, goes at length
The liquor: stuff for strength.

3.

One pours your cup — sheer sweet,
The fragrant fumes of a year condensed:
Suspicion of all that's ripe or rathe,
From the bud on branch to the grass in swathe.
"We suck mere milk of the seasons," saith
A curl of each nostril — "dew, dispensed
Nowise for nerving man to feat:
Boys sip such honeyed sweet!"

4.

And thus who wants wine strong,
Waves each sweet smell of the year away;
Who likes to swoon as the sweets suffuse
His brain with a mixture of beams and dews

Turned sirupy drink — rough strength eschews :
"What though in our veins your wine-stock stay ?
The lack of the bloom does our palate wrong.
Give us wine sweet, not strong ! "

5.

Yet wine is — some affirm —
Prime wine there is in the world somewhere,
Of portable strength with sweet to match.
You double your heart its dose, yet catch —
As the draught descends — a violet-smatch,
Through drops expressed by the fire and worm :
Strong sweet wine — some affirm.

6.

Body and bouquet both?
'Tis easy to ticket a bottle so ;
But what was the case in the cask, my friends?
Cask?   Nay, the vat — where the maker mends

His strong with his sweet (you suppose) and blends

    His rough with his smooth, till none can know

How it comes you may tipple, nothing loath,

    Body and bouquet both.

7.

" You " being just — the world.

    No poets — who turn, themselves, the winch

Of the press ; no critics — I'll even say,

(I am flustered and easy of faith, to-day)

Who for love of the work have learned the way

    Till themselves produce home-made, at a pinch :

No ! You are the world, and wine ne'er purled

    Except to please the world !

8.

" For, oh the common heart !

    And, ah the irremissible sin

Of poets who please themselves, not us !

Strong wine yet sweet wine pouring thus,

How please still — Pindar and Æschylus !—
Drink — dipt into by the bearded chin
Alike and the bloomy lip — no part
    Denied the common heart !

9.

"And might we get such grace,
    And did you moderns but stock our vault
With the true half-brandy half-attar-gul,
How would seniors indulge at a hearty pull
While juniors tossed off their thimbleful !
    Our Shakespeare and Milton escaped your fault,
So, they reign supreme o'er the weaker race
    That want the ancient grace !"

10.

If I paid myself with words
    (As the French say well) I were dupe indeed !
I were found in belief that you quaffed and bowsed
At your Shakespeare the whole day long, caroused

In your Milton pottle-deep nor drowsed

A moment of night — toped on, took heed

Of nothing like modern cream-and-curds !

   Pay me with deeds, not words !

11.

For — see your cellarage !

   There are forty barrels with Shakespeare's brand.

Some five or six are abroach : the rest

Stand spigoted, fauceted. Try and test

What yourselves call best of the very best !

   Why is it that still untouched they stand ?

Why don't you try tap, advance a stage

   With the rest in cellarage ?

12.

For — see your cellarage !

   There are four big butts of Milton's brew.

How comes it you make old drips and drops

Do duty, and there devotion stops ?

Leave such an abyss of malt and hops

  Embellied in butts which bungs still glue ?

You hate your bard ! A fig for your rage !

  Free him from cellarage !

13.

'Tis said I brew stiff drink,

  But the deuce a flavor of grape is there.

Hardly a May-go-down, 'tis just

A sort of a gruff Go-down-it-must —

No Merry-go-down, no gracious gust

  Commingles the racy with May, the rare !

" What wonder," say you " we cough, and blink

  October's heady drink ? "

14.

Is it a fancy, friends ?

  Mighty and mellow are never mixed,

Though mighty and mellow be born at once.

Sweet for the future, — strong for the nonce !

Stuff you should stow away, ensconce

In the deep and dark, to be found fast-fixed

At the century's close: such time strength spends

A-sweetening for my friends!

15.

And then — why, what you quaff

With a smack of lip and a cluck of tongue,

Is leakage and leavings — just what haps

From the tun some learned taster taps

With a promise " Prepare your watery chaps!

Here's properest wine for old and young!

Dispute its perfection — you make us laugh!

Have faith, give thanks, but — quaff!"

16.

Leakage, I say, or worse,

Leavings suffice pot-valiant souls.

Somebody, brimful, long ago,

Frothed flagon he drained to the dregs; and lo,

Down whisker and beard what an overflow !
  Lick spilth that has trickled from classic jowls.
Sup the single scene, sip the only verse —
  Old wine, not new and worse !

17.

I grant you : worse by much !
  Renounce that new where you never gained
One glow at heart, one gleam at head,
And stick to the warrant of age instead !
No dwarf's-lap ! Fatten, by giants fed !
  You fatten, with oceans of drink undrained?
You feed — who would choke did a cobweb smutch
  The Age you love so much ? .   ⸴

18.

A mine's beneath a moor :
  Acres of moor roof fathoms of mine
Which diamonds dot where you please to dig :
Yet who plies spade for the bright and big ?

Your product is — truffles, you hunt with a pig !

Since bright-and-big, when a man would dine,

Suies badly: and therefore the Koh-i-noor

May sleep in mine 'neath moor !

19.

Wine, pulse in might from me !

It may never emerge in must from vat,

Never fill cask nor furnish can,

Never end sweet, which strong began —

God's gift to gladden the heart of man ;

But spirit's at proof, I promise that !

No sparing of juice spoils what should be

Fit brewage — mine for me.

20.

Man's thoughts and loves and hates !

Earth is my vineyard, these grew there :

From grape of the ground, I made or marred

My vintage ; easy the task or hard,

Who set it — his praise be my reward !
    Earth's yield !   Who yearn for the Dark Blue Sea's
Let them "lay, pray, bray" — the addle-pates,
    Mine be Man's thoughts, loves, hates !

21.

But some one says "Good Sir !"
    ('Tis a worthy versed in what concerns
The making such labor turn out well)
"You don't suppose that the nosegay-smell
Needs always come from the grape ?   Each bell
    At your foot, each bud that your Honor spurns,
The very cowslip would act like myrrh
    On the stiffest brew — good Sir !

22.

"Cowslips, abundant birth
    O'er meadow and hillside, vineyard too,
— Like a schoolboy's scrawlings in and out
Distasteful lesson-book — all about

Greece and Rome, victory and rout —
Love-verses instead of such vain ado !
So, fancies frolic it o'er the earth
Where thoughts have rightlier birth.

23.

"Nay, thoughtlings they themselves :
Loves, hates — in little and less and least !
Thoughts ? ' *What is a man beside a mount !*'
Loves ? ' *Absent — poor lovers the minutes count !*'
Hates ? ' *Fie — Pope's letters to Martha Blount !*'
These furnish a wine for a children's-feast :
Insipid to man, they suit the elves
Like thoughts, loves, hates themselves."

24.

And, friends, beyond dispute
I too have the cowslips dewy and dear.
Punctual as Springtide forth peep they :
I leave them to make my meadow gay.

But I ought to pluck and impound them, eh?
　　Not let them alone, but deftly shear
And shred and reduce to — what may suit
　　Children, beyond dispute?

25

And, here's May-month, all bloom,
　　All bounty : what if I sacrifice?
If I out with shears and shear, nor stop
Shearing till prostrate, lo, the crop?
And will you prefer it to ginger-pop
　　When I've made you wine of the memories
Which leave as bare as a churchyard tomb
　　My meadow, late all bloom?

26.

Nay, what ingratitude
　　Should I hesitate to amuse the wits
That have pulled so long at my flask, nor grudged
The headache that paid their pains, nor budged

From bunghole before they sighed and judged
" Too rough for our taste, to-day, befits
The racy and right when the years conclude ! "
Out on ingratitude !

27.

Grateful or ingrate — none,
No cowslip of all my fairy crew
Shall help to concoct what makes you wink,
And goes to your head till you think you think
I like them alive : the printer's ink
Would sensibly tell on the perfume too.
I may use up my nettles, ere I've done ;
But of cowslips — friends get none !

28.

Don't nettles make a broth
Wholesome for blood grown lazy and thick ?
Maws out of sorts make mouths out of taste.
My Thirty-four Port — no need to waste

On a tongue that's fur and a palate — paste !
A magnum for friends who are sound ! the sick —
I'll posset and cosset them, nothing loath,
Henceforward with nettle-broth !